S0-AKZ-306

"A TRIUMPH!"—*Boston Globe*

"STUNNING . . . It is not just the summer of 1939 in a single resort town that he is trying to dramatize, but the entire pre–World War II experience of the Jews in Germany and Austria."

—*The New York Times*

"A SPELLBINDER, very different from any other Holocaust novel . . . harrowing because of its poetic simplicity."   —*Publishers Weekly*

"The most shocking thing about this novel is . . . its charm. Appelfeld manages to treat his appalling theme with grace. The atmosphere is not so much tragic as imbued with a Watteau-like melancholy. The characters [are] funny, sad, helpless *commedia dell'arte* figures."

—*The New York Review of Books*

AHARON APPELFELD was born in Czernovitz, Bukovina, in 1932. In the Nazi sweep east, his mother was killed and he was deported to the labor camp at Transnistria, from which he soon escaped. He was eight years old. For the next three years he wandered the forests. Sometime in 1944 he was picked up by the Red Army, served in field kitchens in the Ukraine, and then made his way to Italy. He reached Palestine in 1946. A veteran of the Israeli Army, married, and the father of three children, he teaches Hebrew literature at Ben-Gurion University of the Negev at Beer Sheva. He is the author of several novels and books of short stories in Hebrew. *Badenheim 1939* is his first book to appear in English.

BADENHEIM 1939

Aharon Appelfeld

WASHINGTON SQUARE PRESS
PUBLISHED BY POCKET BOOKS NEW YORK

A Washington Square Press Publication of
POCKET BOOKS, a Simon & Schuster division of
GULF & WESTERN CORPORATION
1230 Avenue of the Americas, New York, N.Y. 10020

Copyright © 1980 by Aharon Appelfeld

Published by arrangement with David R. Godine, Publishers, Inc.
Library of Congress Catalog Card Number: 80-66192

All rights reserved, including the right to reproduce
this book or portions thereof in any form whatsoever.
For information address David R. Godine, Publishers, Inc.
306 Dartmouth Street, Boston, Mass. 02116

ISBN: 0-671-43592-2

First Washington Square Press printing November, 1981

10 9 8 7 6 5 4 3 2 1

WASHINGTON SQUARE PRESS, WSP and colophon are
trademarks of Simon & Schuster.

Printed in the U.S.A.

BADENHEIM 1939

1

Spring returned to Badenheim. In the
country church next to the town the bells rang. The
shadows of the forest retreated to the trees. The sun
scattered the remnants of the darkness and its light
filled the main street from square to square. It was a
moment of transition. The town was about to be
invaded by the vacationers. Two inspectors passed
through an alley, examining the flow of the sewage in
the pipes. The town, which had changed its inhabitants many times in the course of the years, had kept
its modest beauty.

The pharmacist's sick wife, Trude, stood by the
window. She looked around her listlessly with the
gaze of a woman chronically ill. The light fell kindly
on her pale face and she smiled. It had been a
strange, hard winter. Storms had swept through the
town and torn the roofs off the houses. Rumors were
rife. Trude lay in a delirious sleep. Martin never left

her bedside. She spoke constantly of her married daughter, and Martin reassured her that everything was all right. Now the winter was over. She stood by the window as if she had been resurrected from the dead.

The small, well-kept houses put on their tranquil looks again. White islands in a sea of green.

"Has the mail come?"

"Today's Monday. The mail only comes in the afternoon."

The carriage of the impresario, Dr. Pappenheim, suddenly emerged from the forest and came to a stop in the main street. The doctor stepped out of the carriage and waved. No one answered his wave. The street lay in silence.

"Who's arrived?" asked Trude.

"Dr. Pappenheim."

Dr. Pappenheim brought the moist breath of the big city with him, the smell of excitement and anxiety. He would spend his time at the Post Office. Telegrams and express letters would be sent.

Apart from Dr. Pappenheim's arrival, nothing happened. The spring light streamed forth serenely, as it did every year. In the afternoon people gathered in the café and devoured pink ice cream.

"Has the mail come yet?" asked Trude again.

"Yes, but there's nothing for us."

"Nothing." Now you could hear the sickness in her voice. She went back to bed, her forehead burning. Martin took off his coat and sat down beside her.

"Don't worry," he said. "There was a letter only last week. Everything's all right."

But her hallucinations would not leave her: "Why does he beat her?"

"No one beats her. Leopold is a good man and he loves her. What are you thinking of?"

She fell silent, chastised. Martin was tired. He put his head on the pillow and fell asleep.

The next morning the first guests arrived. The front window of the pastry shop was decorated with flowers. In the hotel gardens the following people appeared: Dr. Shutz, Professor Fussholdt and his young wife, and Frau Zauberblit. To Trude they looked not like the familiar vacationers, but like patients in a sanitorium.

"Don't you recognize Professor Fussholdt?" asked Martin.

"They look very pale to me."

"They've just come from the city," said Martin, trying to distract her. Now Martin knew that his wife was very ill. The drugs would not help. The whole world looked transparent to her. It was poisoned and diseased; their married daughter, captive and abused. His attempts to reassure her were in vain. She had stopped listening. That night Martin sat down and wrote a letter to his daughter Helena. Spring in Badenheim was delightful. The first guests had arrived. But her mother missed her very much.

Trude's illness seeped into his soul drop by drop. He too began to see patches of paleness on people's faces. Since Helena's marriage everything in the house had changed. For a whole year they had tried to stop her, but nothing had helped. She was, as they say, head over heels in love. In the end, a hasty marriage had been arranged.

Spring rose in a dark green haze from the gardens. The two local prostitutes, Sally and Gertie, put on summer dresses and strolled down the avenue. In the beginning the inhabitants of the town had tried to get them thrown out, but the campaign, which began many years ago, had come to nothing in the end. The town had grown used to them, as it had grown used to Dr. Pappenheim's eccentricities and to the foreigners who had insinuated themselves like diseased roots. Only the pastry shop owner was adamant. He would not allow them to cross his threshold, and they were thus deprived of the best cream cakes in the world. The boyish Dr. Shutz, who had a soft spot for Sally, once took some cakes out to them in the avenue. The pastry owner found out, and there was a scandal. But his battle too was in vain.

"And how are the ladies?" asked Dr. Pappenheim gallantly.

In the course of time they had lost their city airs, bought themselves a little house, and begun to dress like the local girls. At the beginning they gave wild parties. But the years and the mistresses from the city had pushed them aside. Without their savings they would have been in a bad way. All they had left were their memories, and like widows on long winter nights they would bring them up from their graves.

"What's happened this year?"

"Nothing out of the ordinary," said Dr. Pappenheim cheerfully.

"A strange winter, wasn't it?"

They were fond of Dr. Pappenheim and over the years they had even begun to take an interest in his strange artists. In their long exile they clutched at any straw that offered itself.

"Not to worry, not to worry! The Festival program's full of surprises this year!"

"Who's it going to be this time?"

"A yanuka, a child prodigy. I discovered him in Vienna in the winter."

"A yanuka," said Sally in a maternal voice.

By the next day Badenheim was already flooded with vacationers. The hotel was a hive of activity. The spring light and the laughter of the people filled the streets, and in the hotel gardens the porters once more carried the brightly colored baggage. Dr. Pappenheim seemed to shrink. His timetable was in a muddle. He rushed from place to place. For years the artists had been driving him crazy and now they wanted to ruin him altogether.

The people left their baggage in the hotel and streamed toward the forest. Professor Fussholdt and his young wife. A tall man ceremoniously leading Frau Zauberblit. "Why don't we go left?" said Frau Zauberblit, and everybody turned to the left. Dr. Shutz followed them as if spellbound.

"Why do they walk so slowly?" asked Trude.

"Why, because they're on vacation, of course," said Martin, as if nothing could be simpler.

"Who's the man walking next to Frau Zauberblit? Isn't it her brother?"

"No, my dear. Her brother's been dead for years."

2

That night the band arrived. Dr. Pappenheim was as happy as if a miracle had taken place.
The porters unloaded the trumpets and drums. The
musicians stood by the gate like tame birds on a
stick. Dr. Pappenheim distributed candy. The van
driver urged the porters on, and the musicians ate
and said nothing.

"Why are you late?" asked Dr. Pappenheim, with
a certain feeling of relief.

"The van came late."

The conductor, who was wearing a tailored cloak,
stood to one side as if it all had nothing to do with
him. During the past year he had been waging a
bitter struggle with Dr. Pappenheim. Pappenheim
had considered firing him, but the senior musicians
took their conductor's side and nothing came of it.
The conductor demanded a detailed three-year con-

tract on the usual terms. In the end, they reached a compromise.

Previously Dr. Pappenheim had housed the musicians in small, dark rooms on the ground floor of the hotel. The new contract held a clause specifying that there were entitled to decent living quarters. Now they were all waiting to see their rooms. Pappenheim went up to the conductor and whispered in his ear: "The rooms are ready. Spacious, airy rooms on the top floor."

"Sheets?" asked the conductor.

"Sheets too."

Pappenheim had kept his promise. The rooms were fine. At the sight of the rooms the musicians hastily took off their clothes and put on their blue uniforms. Dr. Pappenheim stood to one side and made no attempt to hurry them. In one of the rooms a little quarrel broke out, a quarrel about a bed. The conductor reprimanded them: such fine rooms demanded quiet. And before they went down they must put all their things away.

At ten o'clock everything was ready. The musicians stood in threes with their instruments in their hands. But Pappenheim could not contain his indignation. If only he had the money he would pay them off and tell them to go to hell. More than anything they reminded him of his failures. Thirty years. Always late. Never rehearsed. All they knew how to do was make a noise. And every year new demands.

The evening began. The people buzzed around the band like bees. The musicians blew their horns and beat their drums as if they would have liked to drive them all away. Dr. Pappenheim sat in the gallery and downed stein after stein of beer.

The next day everything was quiet and relaxed.

14

Martin rose early, swept the entrance, wiped the shelves, and drew up a detailed stock order. He had had a hard night. Trude would not be pacified. She refused to take her medicine, and in the end he was obliged to deceive her and slip her a sleeping pill on the sly.

At about ten o'clock an inspector from the Sanitation Department appeared with orders to carry out an inspection. He wanted to know all kinds of peculiar details. The ownership of the business, if Martin had inherited it, when and from whom he had acquired it, how much it was worth. Martin, surprised, explained that everything had been whitewashed and thoroughly disinfected. The inspector took out a yardstick and measured. He left abruptly without apologizing or thanking Martin.

Martin was upset by the visit. He believed in the authorities and blamed himself as a matter of course. Perhaps the back entrance had been neglected. The abrupt visit spoiled his morning. He stood on the lawn. A morning like any other. The milkman made his way down the street with his heavy peasant's walk, the musicians came out into the garden. Pappenheim did not bother them and they lay about sunbathing on the lawn. The conductor sat in a corner dealing cards to himself. In the afternoon Frau Zauberblit appeared in the pharmacy and announced that there was nothing like a holiday in Badenheim. She was wearing a polka-dot poplin dress. But to Martin it seemed that her dead brother was standing just behind her.

"Isn't it strange?" he asked.

"Everything's possible," she said, as if she understood his question.

Martin was angry; it was all Trude's fault.

15

The musicians spent the whole afternoon lying around in the garden. Without their uniforms they looked unimpressive. For years they had been arguing with Pappenheim. Now they argued among themselves. The conductor did not interfere. He laid out the cards and looked at them. One of the musicians, with a very tough expression on his face, took a pay slip out of his vest pocket and showed it to his friends. The other musicians demonstrated to him that he was wrong. From Martin's garden it all looked like a mirage, perhaps because of the fading light and the lengthening shadows falling one after another onto the green grass.

When it grew dark the conductor gestured to the musicians to go upstairs and put on their uniforms. They moved off slowly, like soldiers worn out by long service. The conductor exchanged a few words with Pappenheim. Dr. Pappenheim expounded on the Festival program at length.

"I heard that Mandelbaum's coming too. An extraordinary achievement. How did you manage it?"

"I worked like a horse," said Dr. Pappenheim, and turned toward the dining room.

The guests were already guzzling. The waitress kept looking sharply in the direction of the kitchen: the orders were not arriving in time. But the older waiters praised the food cynically with an affected air of self-importance.

Trude's condition did not improve. Martin talked and talked, but his words did not help. Everything looked transparent and diseased to her. Helena was a captive on Leopold's estate and every evening when he returned from the barracks he beat her.

"Can't you see it for yourself?" she asked.

"No, I can't."

"So it's all my delusions then."

Martin was irritated. Trude was always talking about her parents, about the little house on the banks of the Vistula. Her parents were dead. The connection with her brothers had been broken. Martin said that she was still stuck in that world, in the mountains among the Jews. And, in a sense, he was right. She was haunted by a hidden fear, not her own, and Martin felt that he was becoming infected by her hallucinations.

3

The next day the public was informed that the jurisdiction of the Sanitation Department had been extended, and that it had been authorized to conduct independent investigations. A modest announcement to this effect was posted on the municipal notice board. With the publication of the announcement, the inspectors spread out and, without ceremony, began investigating the places marked on their maps. The investigations were carried out scrupulously, in accordance with questionnaires that had arrived from the district office. One of the musicians, who bore his Polish name with a peculiar pride, said that the inspectors reminded him of marionettes in a play. His name was Leon Samitzky. Fifty years ago, when he was a child, his parents had emigrated from Poland. He remembered the scenes of his childhood with a surreptitious affection. Sometimes, when the spirit moved him, he would sit and talk about Poland. And Dr. Pappenheim, who enjoyed his stories, would sit and listen like one of the musicians.

The clouds melted and the spring sunlight poured forth its warmth. A secret worry crept over the faces of the aging musicians. They sat together without speaking.

Suddenly Samitzky broke the silence and said, "I'm homesick for Poland."

"Why?" asked Pappenheim.

"I don't know," said Samitzky. "When I left Poland I was seven years old, and now it seems to me that it was only a year ago."

"The people are very poor there," said someone in a whisper.

"They may be poor, but they're not afraid of death."

That evening nothing happened in Badenheim. Dr. Pappenheim was sunk in melancholy. He could not take his eyes off Samitzky. He too remembered the rare visits of his grandmother from the Carpathians. She was a big, broad woman and when she came to Vienna she brought with her the smell of forests and millet fields. His father hated her.

Rumors were rife. Some said that it was nothing but a health hazard, which the inspectors were trying to locate; others thought they were the Income Tax collectors in disguise. The musicians traded guesses. The town itself remained calm and cooperated with the authorities, giving the Sanitation Department whatever it asked for. Even the proud pastry shop owner filled out the questionnaire without making a fuss. In the meantime the pale vacationers invaded the pastry shop. The owner could not keep up with the demand. This year their hunger knew no bounds. They snapped up whatever they could get. The owner goaded the pastry cook. The oven roared all day long. The cakes were snatched up while they were still hot. "Have another one. . . . Why don't you have another one? . . . Wild horses couldn't drag me out of here. . . . " For hours the intoxicated words flew through the air. The people stayed until after midnight.

The pastry shop owner tried to calm them down, but it was beyond his power. Appetite and energy conspired against him. The year before, a tall, slender, good-looking woman had appeared in Badenheim. After a few days she had disappeared into the forest. When she returned she put on a bathing suit and went out onto the balcony crying, "I'm free! Free forever!" She no longer belonged to the people but to the scents of the forest, and there was a cold light of madness burning in her eyes.

Such was spring in Badenheim. There was a secret intoxication in the air. Respectable businessmen did not bring their wives here, but anyone who had breathed the air and been infected could not keep away. Every spring they came back like horses to the stable. Here you could find a schoolgirl who had run away from school, a man with a jaunty manner and a haggard face whose mind was worn out with books, and tall women to whose brows vague secrets clung like skin.

"Is it possible to send a letter from here?" asked a woman.

"Of course," said Dr. Pappenheim.

"That's strange," said the woman. "I thought the place was completely isolated."

The musicians went down to the bar to have a beer. Years in the service of Dr. Pappenheim at holiday resorts had sucked them dry. Without drink their lives weren't worth living. At the beginning the conductor had deprived them of this little pleasure, but in recent years he had taken to urging them to go down to the bar and have a drink. The beer made them more cheerful. Of rehearsals, he had quite despaired. Even Pappenheim had almost ceased demanding rehearsals.

The year before, the band had suddenly broken into Jewish melodies, to the annoyance of the regular guests. They themselves apparently did not know what they were playing. Perhaps they remembered the tunes from long ago, or perhaps they had heard them somewhere. The beer was ruining them. They grew fat, guzzled without stopping, and at the end of the season they were always in debt.

"They're incorrigible," said Pappenheim.

The waitress, who was only half Jewish, was kind to them and called them "children." When the headwaiter was resting or had the day off, she would ply them with delicacies.

4

The inspectors of the Sanitation Department were now spread all over the town. They took measurements, put up fences, and planted flags. Porters unloaded rolls of barbed wire, cement pillars, and all kinds of appliances suggestive of preparations for a public celebration.

"There'll be fun and games this year."

"How do you know?"

"The Festival's probably going to be a big affair this year; otherwise, why would the Sanitation Department be going to all this trouble?"

"You're right, I didn't realize."

The south gate was closed and another gate, which had been shut for generations, was opened for pedestrians. The officials of the Sanitation Department worked day and night, with a tapping of hammers and a glare of projectors. "Dr. Pappenheim's making a name for himself at last," said one of the old-timers, who had once expressed doubts about Pappenheim's abilities as an impresario.

Mild, temperate breezes began to blow making everyone feel healthy and restored. Hammocks went up in the gardens and nets in the tennis courts. People took off their winter clothes and put on sport shirts. Martin withdrew into himself. People bought everything they could lay their hands on. The cosmetic counter was empty. The new orders came late. If it hadn't been for his stocks he would have had nothing to sell. The town, which had been through a long winter with hard rains, now throbbed with a hectic, feverish gaiety.

All day long the impresario sat by the telephone. The artists did not contact him, did not reply to his letters, did not keep their promises. How would he keep to his schedule? The patrons would demand their money back, and rightly. For the moment, it was his worry. The people were caught up in their own rejoicing and in the spring, which drew them deep into the thick forests. But Dr. Pappenheim knew that after this enthusiasm they would fall on him and demand their money's worth. "The artists, the artists!" they would cry. He stood in the Post Office and sent one telegram after another: save me, rescue me, you can't leave me in the lurch like this. The telegrams went off into the distance, but there were no replies.

And in the pastry shop they drank coffee and devoured cakes. One of the musicians, a wit, calculated that the pastry shop owner would make a fortune this year. The guests were investing their money in strawberry tarts. The pastry shop owner was pleased, but his satisfaction was not complete. The pastry cook was lazy, a malingerer, and he himself had to work all night long to keep up with the demand.

After midnight Dr. Pappenheim arrived in the pastry shop. The people were already half asleep. One of the old musicians, who was afraid of losing his job, sat down next to him and said that the vacationers were very impressed by the extent of the preparations this year. He was sure that they were in for a lot of surprises. No one would dare laugh at Badenheim anymore. Pappenheim knew this was only the flattery of an old musician afraid of losing his job, but he did not snub him. He was tired and hungry. The man's voice dripped into him like raindrops pattering into an empty barrel.

5

At the end of April the two readers arrived. Dr. Pappenheim put on his blue suit in their honor. They were tall and thin and had a monkish look. Rilke was their passion. Dr. Pappenheim, who had discovered them in Vienna, immediately sensed the morbid melody throbbing in their voices and was fascinated. This was seven years ago, maybe even more, and ever since then he had been unable to do without them. At first the response to their reading was not enthusiastic, but once the people had discovered the hidden melody in their voices they were intoxicated. Now Frau Zauberblit breathed a sigh of relief: they had arrived.

The readers were twin brothers who during the course of the years had become indistinguishable. But the way they read was different; it was as if their sickness had two voices. The voice of the first was soft and conciliatory; it was less a voice than the remnants of a voice. The second's voice was clear and sharp. Frau Zauberblit said that if it hadn't been for their double voice, her life would be pointless. She loved their reading. It was like a healing potion to her, and in the empty spring nights she whispered Rilke to herself.

The musicians, who played in dance halls in the winter and holiday resorts in the summer, could not understand what the people found in these morbid voices. Pappenheim tried in vain to explain their fascination. Only Samitzky said that their voices touched his infected cells. The conductor hated them and called them "the clowns of the modern age."

And in the meantime the spring worked its magic. Dr. Shutz followed the schoolgirl around like a lovesick boy. Frau Zauberblit was deep in long discussions with Samitzky, and Professor Fussholdt's young wife put on a bathing suit and sunbathed on the lawn.

The twins rehearsed all the time. Apparently they couldn't manage without rehearsal. "And I in my innocence thought that with them it all just came out," said Frau Zauberblit.

"Practicing, practicing," said Samitzky. "If only I'd practiced like them in my youth I wouldn't have landed up in this pathetic outfit. I wasn't born here. I was born in Poland, and my parents didn't provide me with a musical education." After midnight Dr. Pappenheim received a telegram saying that Mandelbaum had been taken ill and would not be able to keep his engagement. Dr. Pappenheim stood up, shook his head, and said, "A catastrophe."

"Mandelbaum!" said Frau Zauberblit.

"The artistic Festival is falling apart," said Pappenheim. Samitzky tried to console them, but Pappenheim said, "Mandelbaum was the crowning event." He sunk into his sorrow like a stone. Frau Zauberblit ordered the French wine that Pappenheim liked but he didn't touch it, and all night long he lamented, "Mandelbaum, Mandelbaum."

6

And the investigations showed what reality was. From now on nobody would be able to say that the Sanitation Department was inefficient. Estrangement, suspicion, and mistrust began to invade the town. But the people were still preoccupied with their own affairs—the guests with their pleasures and the townspeople with their troubles. Dr. Pappenheim could not stop lamenting the loss of Mandelbaum. Ever since the telegram his life wasn't worth living. Professor Fussholdt's young wife announced that something had changed in Badenheim. Professor Fussholdt did not leave his room. His crowning work was about to be published and he was busy working on the proofs. His young wife, whom he pampered like a kitten, understood nothing about his work. Her only interests were clothes and cosmetics. In the hotel they called her Mitzi.

In the middle of May a modest announcement

appeared on the notice board saying that all citizens who were Jews had to register with the Sanitation Department no later than the end of the month.

"That means me," said Samitzky.

"And me," said Pappenheim. "Surely you don't want to deny me my Jewishness?"

"I'd like to," said Samitzky, "but your nose testifies to the fact that you're no Austrian."

The conductor, who had grown accustomed over the years to blaming Pappenheim for everything that went wrong, said, "Because of him I had to go and get mixed up in this bureaucratic mess. The officials have gone out of their minds and I have to suffer."

People began avoiding Dr. Pappenheim like the plague, but he did not sense their hostility and went on rushing back and forth as usual between the hotel and the Post Office.

Over the past two weeks Trude's illness had grown worse. She spoke about death all the time, no longer in fear but with a kind of intimacy. The strong drugs she continued to take carried her from sleep to sleep, and to Martin it seemed that she was wandering through other phases of her life.

People began unburdening themselves to each other as if they were speaking of an old illness which there was no longer any point in hiding, and their reactions were different: shame and pride. Frau Zauberblit said nothing and asked no questions, maintaining a pose of deliberate indifference. In the end she approached Samitzky and asked, "Have you registered?"

"Not yet," said Samitzky. "I'm waiting for the right opportunity. Do I have the honor of addressing an Austrian citizen of Jewish origin?"

"You do, sir."

"In that case we shall soon be able to hold a family celebration."

"Did you ever doubt it?"

The headwaiter himself served the cherries of the season, white cherries. The lilac bushes climbed the verandah railings and the bees greedily devoured the blue flowers. Frau Zauberblit tied a silk scarf around her straw hat. The cherries had come straight from Waldenheim that very morning; they had ripened early this year. "Isn't that wonderful!" said Frau Zauberblit. She adored these rustic touches.

"What are you thinking about?" asked Samitzky.

"I'm thinking about my grandfather's house. He was the rabbi of Kirchenhaus, a man of God. I used to spend my summer holidays with him. He used to go out in the evenings to walk by the river. He loved nature."

Samitzky drank heavily. "Don't worry, children. We'll be going to Poland soon. Just imagine—Poland."

Dr. Shutz ran around like a madman. The schoolgirl was driving him crazy. "Dr. Shutz, why don't you join intelligent company for some intelligent conversation?" said Frau Zauberblit. In academic circles he was considered a genius, although something of an *enfant terrible*.

"Have you registered?" asked Samitzky.

"What?" said Shutz, surprised.

"You have to register. Haven't you heard? According to the regulations of the Sanitation Department. A fine department, a government department whose jurisdiction has been extended in recent months—this department earnestly requests the registration of Dr. Shutz."

"It's no joke, my dear," said Frau Zauberblit.

"Is that so?" said Shutz, completely at a loss. He was the spoiled darling of Badenheim. Everybody loved him. Pappenheim never stopped bewailing his wasted musical talents. He was an incorrigible wastrel whose rich old mother paid his debts at the end of every season.

A distant dread settled in the eyes of the musicians. "What's there to worry about?" said Dr. Pappenheim bracingly. "Enough of this gloom."

"We're visitors here, aren't we? Do we have to register too?" asked one of the musicians.

"I should say," said Dr. Pappenheim impressively, "that the Sanitation Department wants to boast of its important guests and is thus writing their names down in its Golden Book. Isn't that handsome of them?"

"Maybe it's all because of the *Ostjuden,*" said one of the musicians.

At this point Samitzky stood up and proclaimed: "What's the matter, don't you like me? I'm an *Ostjude,* in the full sense of the word. Have you got anything against me?"

7

Badenheim's intoxicating spring was playing havoc with the vacationers again. Dr. Shutz was left without a penny to his name and sent two express letters to his mother. The schoolgirl was apparently costing him a fortune. Frau Zauberblit sat with Samitzky all day long. It seemed that this man was all that was left her in the world. Dr. Pappenheim was sunk in gloom; the spring always made him sad. Frau Zauberblit scolded him and said: "I'll cover the losses. Just make out an account. If Mandelbaum keeps on playing tricks on you, I'll get Kraus's chamber ensemble." The twins wandered about the town, a secret branded on their brows. In the hotel they were spoken of as invalids, in whispers. They ate nothing, and drank coffee all day long.

The headwaiter said: "If I could serve them

Rilke's Death Sonnets maybe they would eat. It seems they can't digest any other kind of food."

After breakfast Frau Zauberblit, Dr. Pappenheim, and Samitzky made up their minds to go and register at the Sanitation Department. The official did not bat an eye at Zauberblit's declarations. She praised the department and said there was nothing like it for order and beauty. No wonder they had been promoted. Samitzky announced that his parents had arrived here fifty years ago and he had never since stopped feeling homesick. The official wrote down the required information expressionlessly like a stenographer.

That night Samitzky did not wear his uniform. The band played. And everyone saw plainly that Frau Zauberblit had a new admirer. She was radiant, like a woman in love. Professor Fussholdt's young wife was going out of her mind. Her husband was immersed in his new book and did not stir from his desk. She was sick of the people in Badenheim. What was there to do here? Poetry readings again. They put her into a depression. One of the musicians, a cynic, told her not to upset herself. In Poland everything was beautiful, everything was interesting.

The next day Trude roused the street with her screams. The hotel guests stood on the verandah and watched the desperate struggle. No one went down to help. Poor Martin, helpless, knelt at her feet and implored her: "Calm yourself, Trude, calm yourself. There's no forest here. There are no wolves here."

A strange night descended on Badenheim. The cafés were deserted and the people walked the streets silently. There was something unthinking about their movements, as if they were being led. It was as if some alien spirit had descended on the town. Dr. Shutz led the tall schoolgirl as if he would have liked to chain her to him. Sally and Gertie walked hand in hand, like young girls.

The dewy light of spring nights settled softly on the pavements. The musicians sat on the verandah and surveyed the town with sharp, nervous looks. The solitary Dr. Pappenheim sat in a corner and calculated sadly to himself: the trio had betrayed him. The people would never forgive him. And they would be right. If only he had known, he would have designed the whole program differently.

8

Once more the month of May played havoc with the trees. The pavements were covered with a snowfall of blossoms. The sun shone down from its skied highway and strayed in the alleys. The shadows of the forest retreated and left the town to the light. The first intoxication died down. A woman remembered that far from here she had left a home. What was she doing here? Who had seduced her?

"The local line passes not far from here," explained Martin, pointing out the direction to her. "It stops at night."

"Is there no direct bus, no direct train?" the woman asked despairingly.

Dr. Pappenheim cajoled, explained: all he needed was a little time. The artists would show up in the end. They always did. But what good were words? The first fear, the fear that always came with the scents of spring, had struck at the hearts of the people.

"Stay here," a man's voice said.

The woman listened for a moment, and then she said: "What's there to keep me here? I can't understand what's so wonderful about this place."

"The Festival, the Festival. Surely you don't want to miss the Festival?"

At the sound of the magic word she inclined her head as if she were listening not to the seductive words of a man, but to a voice coming to her from far away.

"Where does it take place?" she asked, and immediately regretted the question, which might be interpreted as some kind of agreement on her part.

"In the hall, the big hall."

"I'm not staying here," said the woman and began walking away.

"You can't imagine how wonderful it is. The great artists who come here, the atmosphere . . ."

"Show me the way to the train. I'm not asking you for anything. Just show me the way to the train."

"But it's night. Everything's dark."

"Why did you bring me here?"

"Believe me," said the man in an imploring tone of voice, "I had no evil intentions. I wanted to give you an artistic experience."

"I don't need any artistic experiences. I want to go back to town."

"I'd advise you to stay and hear just one artist. You can go back after that. It would be a pity to miss such an impressive experience."

Strangely enough, the last sentence convinced her. She turned to look at him and said not a word.

"Believe me," he repeated and said no more.

They went into the pastry shop. The cakes, the rustic furniture, the steam of the coffee were more effective than words. He told her about the artists, about Mandelbaum, about the wonderful impresario Dr. Pappenheim, the patron of aspiring artists.

His name was Karl; hers Lotte. Lotte's husband had been the head agent for a big firm. He had lost his life in the mountains. Karl was divorced. His children lived with their grandfather, a retired general, in Berlin. Every day he made them run on the lawn. He wanted to send them to a military academy. The oldest, said Karl, was a sensitive, melancholy lad. How would he be able to stand it? What would he do there? "What can I do? Their mother's a Prussian, born and bred."

Lotte listened silently. Karl was a little sorry that he had unburdened these sad thoughts to her. He looked for other words, but for some reason he could not find them. After a few moments of silence he said, "You can't imagine the feeling of vitality that a stay in Badenheim gives you. I'm very glad that you decided to stay. It's an event not to be missed."

"An event?" said Lotte.

"I can't think of a better word. You're sensitive to words, I see."

Outside there was a new wave of blossoming, purple blossoms which fell slowly to the ground and gave off a pungent scent. The dogs broke out of the bushes and Lotte recoiled with a scream. Karl hugged her and laughed. "Don't be afraid," he said, "they're big dogs but very quiet. They must have been hunting dogs once, but now they're absolutely tame. They're very friendly and they like to be petted."

AHARON APPELFELD

"I've never seen so many dogs together," said Lotte.

"Only four. They're quite tame, there's no trace of their former life left in them."

Suddenly Lotte knew that everything in her life up to now was dead and gone forever. She was not happy. A dull sorrow choked her.

"Go to sleep now," said Karl and the dogs slunk back into the bushes.

The musicians were already drumming rhythmically in the hall. The people were waltzing with sweeping movements. Karl took Lotte by the arm and led her in without ceremony, like a man leading a woman he has known for a long time.

9

The Sanitation Department now resembled a travel agency festooned with posters: LABOR IS OUR LIFE . . . THE AIR IN POLAND IS FRESHER . . . SAIL ON THE VISTULA . . . THE DEVELOPMENT AREAS NEED YOU . . . GET TO KNOW THE SLAVIC CULTURE. These and other slogans adorned the walls.

Frau Zauberblit was as gay as a young girl in love. She laughed at Samitzky's accent and said that from now on he would be their guide. A few weeks before she had escaped from the sanitorium. It was in the afternoon, after the doctors had made their rounds, taken her temperature, measured the amount of blood in her phlegm, and written everything down on her chart. The guards on the ground floor had fallen asleep and death, Death himself, plain and undisguised, appeared and stood in the corridor next to the basin. For a moment she looked at him, like a woman looking at an old lover suddenly reappearing on her doorstep. Then she stood up, got dressed, made up her face, put on her straw hat, and went to the railway station. During the journey she already felt that everything was changing. And when the train stopped in Badenheim and she met her old acquaintances and saw the familiar carriages, death suddenly left her. And she was no longer in pain.

Every year a few patients ran away and every year they came back again. The sanitorium would not let them go. It was an old sanitorium, very formal. The regime was strict but not unpleasant. They held receptions for new patients, once a week the priest came to hear confession, there were friendships and hostilities just like everywhere else. The sanitorium grounds were like a spacious seashore. Death strolled there freely, in the rose garden and the lounge, and they spoke to him as if they were speaking to a tame animal, laughingly and cajoling. And when their time came they departed from the world, some screaming and some silent.

Frau Zauberblit felt laughter, appetite, the desire to wander in the woods returning to her as of old. Samitzky did not understand what she was talking about. The long years in the band had blunted his feelings. He had learned to drink, sleep, and beat the drums. He was always in debt. And now the illustrious Frau Zauberblit called him her prince, and laughed at his broken German, and said that Poland was the most beautiful country of all, and that Yiddish was a lovely, melodious language.

The Sanitation Department was open at night too. Its doors were framed with lights; inside there were journals, posters, and leaflets about agriculture and industry, art and entertainment scattered about on the low tables. You could sit in an armchair, listen to music, leaf through a journal, and dream of Poland. The remote, alien Poland began to seem an idyllic, pastoral place.

"Wouldn't you like to come with us to Poland?" asked Karl.

Lotte's sad look softened. She looked at him fondly and said, "If you like."

The waitress stood at the hotel door urging at the top of her voice: "Why don't you come to us? There aren't too many guests this year and we'll spoil you like orphans." She called the people "esteemed ladies and gentlemen, illustrious guests of Badenheim," and when Dr. Pappenheim appeared she curtsied down to the ground and said, "the impresario in person." The impresario was not as cheerful as the waitress, but he would wipe his worries from his face for a moment and pinch her cheek. And she would cry, "Oh!" The afternoons were spent in the bar or the pastry shop. If it hadn't been for the musicians guzzling themselves sick and then sinking into heavy gloom and melancholy, things would have been more pleasant. But the musicians had seen a lot in their lives and they were braided to what they knew like roots in heavy soil.

10

Three special investigators from the district office turned up at the Sanitation Department. The conductor had an interesting document in his vest pocket. His parents' baptismal certificates. Dr. Pappenheim, surprised, said, "I would never have believed it." Strangely enough, the conductor did not seem happy.

"If the conductor so desires, he could join the Jewish Order, a very fine order indeed," said Pappenheim.

"I don't believe in religion."

"If the conductor so desires, he could be a Jew without religion."

"Who said so? The Sanitation Department?"

In the afternoon it poured. The people gathered in the lobby. Later on they served hot wine, as if it were autumn. Dr. Pappenheim was immersed in a game of chess with Samitzky. In the evening Frau

Zauberblit's daughter arrived. From her father,
General Von Schmidt, she had inherited a straight
back, flaxen hair, pink cheeks, and a harsh voice.
She attended a girls' lycée far from her mother.

General Von Schmidt was still remembered in
Badenheim. They had come here together the first
year after their marriage. But Von Schmidt couldn't
stand the place and called it Pappenheim, after the
impresario. He thought it was a place for sick
people, not healthy ones. There were no horses, no
hunting, and even the beer wasn't real beer. After
this they had stopped coming. Their memory faded.
They had a daughter. The years went by and Von
Schmidt, who had begun his army career as a junior
officer, climbed steadily up the military hierarchy.
The divorce was not slow to follow. After the
divorce Frau Zauberblit appeared in Badenheim
alone—tall, thin, and suffering. And that was the
end of the affair.

The daughter announced immediately that she
had brought a document. It was a legal form re-
nouncing what were referred to as "maternal
rights." Frau Zauberblit examined the form and
asked, "Is this what you want, too?"

"What my father wants and what I want, too," she
replied, as if she were repeating something she had
learned by heart. Frau Zauberblit sighed. The parting was hard and cold. "Excuse me, I'm in a hurry,"
said the girl and left abruptly. The hotel was struck
dumb by the daughter's appearance. Frau Zauberblit sat in a corner without uttering a word. At that
moment a new kind of pride seemed to be growing
on her face.

In the hotel and its wings a secret seemed to be
drawing the people together. The conductor ap-

peared ill at ease and went to sit with the musicians. That evening the twins were to perform. The hotel owner had made the small hall ready. They had not been seen on the verandah for two days. They were in seclusion. "What are they doing up there?" someone asked. The headwaiter confirmed that for two days they had eaten nothing. The people stood next to the windows and the evening light flickered on their faces.

Pappenheim said in a stage whisper, "They're rehearsing. They're fantastic."

In the evening the small hall filled with a worshipful silence. The people came early and Pappenheim rushed from door to door as if it were in his power to bring the performers down before they were due. At eight o'clock they came downstairs and took up their positions by the little table. Pappenheim retired and stood by the door like a sentinel.

For two hours they sat and spoke of death. Their voices were dispassionate. They were like people who had visited hell and were no longer afraid of it. When the reading was over they stood up. The people sat with downcast eyes. There was no applause. Pappenheim approached from the doorway and took off his hat. He looked as if he were about to kneel.

11

In the afternoon apple strudel was served. Frau Zauberblit put on her straw hat, Samitzky wore short tennis pants, and Dr. Pappenheim stood in the doorway like an out-of-work actor. It seemed that the old times had returned and all was calm again.

The day before, at midnight, the yanuka had arrived. The doorman would not let him in on the grounds that his name did not appear on the hotel register. Dr. Pappenheim, who was in a jocular mood, said, "Can't you see that he's a Jew?"

Frau Zauberblit overheard and said, "Everything's going according to plan. Isn't it wonderful?"

"You'll all love him too," said Pappenheim in a low voice.

"The impresario is honoring his obligations. By the way, what language will he sing in?"

"What a question! In Yiddish, of course, in Yiddish!"

Later on, when the yanuka was introduced, the people saw a half-baby, half-boy. There were red patches on his cheeks. His new suit was too big for him.

"What's your name?" Frau Zauberblit approached and asked.

"His name is Nahum Slotzker. And speak slowly," Pappenheim interrupted, "he doesn't understand German."

Suddenly they saw adult lines trembling at the corners of his eyes, but the face was the face of a child. The grown-ups embarrassed him.

"Where are you from? Lodz?" asked Samitzky in Polish.

The boy smiled and said, "From Kalashin."

It was a strange evening. Frau Zauberblit was as gay as a young girl in love. Samitzky paced up and down the corridor like a retired gym teacher. The conductor dealt cards to himself and joked with the waitress, who served him fresh poppy-seed cakes. She was half Jewish and her parents had died when she was young. For a few years she had been the mistress of the Graf Shutzheim. Then the Graf died.

"Will I be allowed to come with you?" she asked slyly.

"What a question! Who'll wait on us in the North if not you?"

"But I'm not fully Jewish."

"And me, am I fully Jewish?"

"Both your parents were Jewish, weren't they?"

"Yes, my dear, they were born Jews, but they converted to Christianity."

The next day Frau Milbaum, the patroness of the twins, arrived. She was a tall, elegant woman with a majestic air. Dr. Pappenheim was overjoyed. Whenever anyone returned it made him happy. The secret was gradually encompassing the people and there was a vague anxiety in the air, born of a new understanding. They walked softly and spoke in whispers. The waiters served strawberries and cream. The summer cast its dark green shade full of intoxicating madness onto the broad verandah. The twins sat blushing by the side of their patroness and did not open their mouths. In company they were like children. Dr. Pappenheim had prepared a full program and the people lived in a strange expectation. Between one investigation and the next the old people died. The town was suffused with strong alcohol fumes. The night before Herr Furst had dropped dead in the café. For years he had strolled the streets, immaculately dressed. And next door, in the casino, another man died next to the roulette wheel. There was a different quality in the air, a sharp clarity which did not come from the local forests.

And in the Sanitation Department the investigations continued quietly. This was now the center, and from the center the net spread out in all directions. In the Sanitation Department they knew everything. They had a large collection of maps, journals, a library. You could drop in whenever you liked and look things up. The conductor went to register and came back happy. They showed him a whole cupboard full of contracts, licenses, and documents. Strange, his old father had written a book about arithmetic in Hebrew. They knew everything, and they were glad to show a man his past, the conductor said.

A barrier was placed at the entrance to the town. No one came in or went out. But the isolation wasn't total. The milkman brought milk in the morning and the fruit truck unloaded its cartons at the hotel. Both cafés remained open and the band played every night, but it still seemed that some other time, from some other place, had invaded the town and was silently establishing itself.

12

And life changed its course: no more forests, walks, picnics, spontaneous or organized excursions. Life was now confined to the hotel, the pastry shop and the swimming pool. The water improved the schoolgirl's figure. She dived expertly and quietly. Dr. Shutz's swimming was noisy and a little heavy. But she did not mock him; she was too absorbed in herself. Sally and Gertie also spent the late morning hours in the swimming pool. At one time this corner had been out of bounds to them, but then the old Graf, who remained loyal, presented each with full membership rights to the pool and the tennis courts. At first the other guests were indignant, but in the end their resentment faded. Sally and Gertie learned to swim, to throw balls in the air, and to enjoy water sports.

In the afternoon people began dropping in at the Sanitation Department. In the souvenir shop a map of Poland was already on sale. The adventurous, full of enthusiasm, spoke of the Vistula and the Carpathian mountains. The first shock was already over. Even the musicians were no longer afraid of asking questions. Only Dr. Langmann was angry: "You must admit, Dr. Pappenheim has really succeeded in waking all the old ghosts from their slumbers."

"What on earth is he talking about?" whispered Karl.

"Is there really any need for explanations now?"

"Perhaps Dr. Langmann would like us to send our children to military academies?"

"What's wrong with young boys engaging in sports?"

"Physical exercise revolts me."

"In that case, why don't you go to Poland, to Lodz, to the *Ostjuden?* Sports revolt them too. They're too busy with their little shops."

"For myself, I can't see anything wrong with little shopkeepers. In my opinion they are far finer than army cadets. At least they don't eat cabbage."

"Just as I said, Pappenheim has awakened the ghosts from their slumbers."

"If you are referring to those little shopkeepers again, let me tell you that I would like to be one of them. I detest sports, hunting makes me sick, my muscles are flabby, my face is pale, I don't eat like a pig, I don't drink beer. Tell me, have you got anything against my way of life?"

"Yes."

"In that case why register here?"

Lotte took no part in the dispute. As if it weren't Karl, whom she had so recently met, talking, but a husband, whose idiosyncrasies she knew like the back of her hand.

In the past they had registered in this same courtyard for organized excursions. In the courtyard next door riding lessons were available. From here too the carriages would set out for the opera, for Karlsheim. Some years ago a man had appeared in the courtyard who afterwards became known by the nickname of "the Bluebird." He was a gaunt man with the face of a monk who preached a Russian version of the Return to Nature. He found a few disciples who went with him to seclude themselves in the mountains. When they returned they told everyone how they had learned to breathe and exercise. They had read passages from the works of Hermann Hesse together. The man evidently knew them by heart.

Over the years this pleasant courtyard had attracted its share of rogues, magicians, and charlatans displaying diplomas of various kinds. Every year had its scandal, and since the appointment of Dr. Pappenheim the scandals had multiplied.

A few years before this very courtyard had witnessed the appearance of a short man dressed in a cheap suit who looked like a traveling salesman. It soon came out, however, that he was not a traveling salesman, but a man traveling with a message. For a few days he stood in the courtyard shouting at passers-by, "Save your souls while there is still time!" He too found a few disciples. But the affair ended scandalously. The man took up with a beautiful schoolgirl and apparently seduced her. Her parents, who came to look for her, sued Dr. Pappenheim and charged him with corrupting the morals of minors.

Now in this same courtyard the people were registering for Poland. The details were obscure.

Pappenheim said jokingly, "What does it matter? What's the difference, here or there? Perhaps our true place really is there." Samitzky was as happy as a boy. The smell of Poland gave him back his childhood. But the others did all they could to escape. The Post Office was flooded with telegrams and express letters and everyone cursed Dr. Pappenheim.

But it soon became clear that there was little to be done. In the hotel they were serving light spring dishes again: cheese dumplings and fresh borscht with sour cream. The headwaiter was cheerful and merry. The half-Jewish waitress pulled the wool over his eyes; at night she plied the hungry musicians with sandwiches and wine.

13

The banquet in honor of the yanuka started late. The people wandered from corridor to corridor and the electric light poured onto their faces. The darkness on the carpets was soft and fuzzy. The waitress served iced coffee. In the hall they set out long tables and covered them with white tablecloths. A few musicians gathered in a corner and played to themselves. Tongues of darkness lapped at the high, narrow windows.

Frau Milbaum sat enthroned in her armchair and her green eyes shot green sparks. People avoided her looks. "Where are my twins?" she murmured. No one answered her. The people were ensnared as if in a net. The twins were chatting to Sally. Sally was wearing a long, flowered dress and gesticulating like a singer. The twins, who were not used to talking to women, laughed in embarrassment.

Sally told them about the first festivals. Gertie appeared and said, "Here you are."

"Allow me to present you to two real gentlemen," said Sally.

The twins held out their long, white hands. The yanuka sat in a corner and did not utter a word. Dr. Pappenheim explained to him in broken Yiddish that the banquet would start soon. The people were waiting to hear his voice.

Everyone was drinking heavily. Frau Milbaum did not stir from her royal throne. Her green eyes were now seething with hate. Her life was full of complications everywhere, and now it was becoming complicated here too. It seemed to her that there was a conspiracy against her. That morning she had registered at the Sanitation Department. The clerk had taken no notice of the aristocratic titles bestowed on her by her first husband, nor had he mentioned her second husband, a nobleman of royal blood. Apart from the name of her father, there was nothing at all on her form.

Sitting on the armchair next to her, Samitzky was chattering away in broken Polish as gaily as a boy. And in his expansiveness he turned to Frau Milbaum and said, "Why don't you join our circle, Madame? You'll find it entertaining, I think."

A steely film covered her eyes. "Thank you," she said.

"Decent company, Jewish aristocracy," he pressed her.

"I understand," she said without looking at him.

"Your company would be an honor," Samitzky pressed her again.

"Don't worry, the Duchess will get used to us," whispered the musician Zimbelman.

"She registered, didn't she? So why so aloof?" someone put in from the corner.

Frau Milbaum surveyed him with her green eyes. "Riffraff!" She finally flung the word out like a stone.

"She's calling us riffraff," said Zimbelman. "Riffraff, she's calling us."

The waitress served cheese and Bordeaux wine. Dr. Pappenheim sat next to the yanuka and encouraged him. "There's nothing to be afraid of. The people are very friendly. You'll stand on the stage and sing."

"I'm afraid," said the child.

"There's nothing to be afraid of; the people are very friendly."

The conductor downed glass after glass. His face grew flushed. "We're going to our native land, Samitzky, we'll have to learn to drink."

"There they drink real alcohol, not beer soup."

"And what will they do there to a goy like me?"

"Don't worry, you've got nothing to fear but circumcision," said Zimbelman, and felt that he had gone a bit too far. "Don't worry, the Jews aren't barbarians, in spite of everything."

Dr. Langmann approached Frau Milbaum and said, "Tomorrow I'm getting out of here."

"Aren't you registered with the Sanitation Department?"

"I still regard myself as a free Austrian citizen. Let them send the Polish Jews to Poland; they deserve their country. I landed in this mess by mistake. Can't a man make an occasional mistake? And the same applies to you. Are we to be deprived of our right to freedom of movement because of a mistake?"

Her look now took in Sally and Gertie. They were

pulling the twins after them into a corner. "Whores," hissed the Duchess. The twins were as happy and excited as a pair of adolescents invited to an orgy.

After midnight they put the child on the stage. He was shaking. Dr. Pappenheim stood next to him with a paternal air. The child sang about the dark forests where the wolf dwelt. It was a kind of lullaby. The musicians surrounded the stage and stared stupidly. Their world was collapsing around them. "Wonderful," said someone.

Samitzky wept drunken tears. Frau Zauberblit went up to him and said, "What is it?"

At the same time Sally was overcome by a hidden fear. She approached Dr. Pappenheim and said, "Dear Dr. Pappenheim, will we too be allowed to go? Will there be room for us too?"

"What are you talking about?" he scolded her. "There's room in our kingdom for all the Jews and for everyone who wants to be a Jew too. Ours is a vast kingdom."

"I'm afraid."

"There's nothing to be afraid of, my dear, we'll all be leaving soon."

Gertie stood to one side and asked no questions, as if she had no right to ask.

14

The summer was at the height of its radiance. Wild roses spread through the drunken gardens and climbed over the fences. Dr. Shutz skipped about like a boy, evoking the schoolgirl's laughter. Lately she had been moody, because of the pool. Swimming in the pool gave her the kind of happiness that only animals know. And now this happiness had been snatched from her. The Sanitation Department had closed the water supply. The schoolgirl pined. Shutz bought her boxes of candy, promised her a tour of the Alps, a trip to Paris, a weekend in Majorca, a sail on the Baltic Sea. He tried everything to make her happy. When he saw that words were useless he skipped like a child, danced like a bear.

Sally and Gertie put on their red skirts and straw hats and set off in the direction of the hotel. Dr. Pappenheim was standing at the door.

"We're being deprived of the pleasures of life," declared Sally.

"What are you talking about?" asked Dr. Pappenheim, surprised.

"They've closed the swimming pool."

"In that case," said Dr. Pappenheim, "we'll have time to study."

They laughed. "Won't you come down to the bar with us? Wouldn't you like a little Malaga?" said Sally.

"I'm ready for anything."

In the bar everyone was having a good time. The musicians had brought the waitress down with them, the half-Jewish waitress. She was cavorting on the stage like a dancer, exposing her legs and saying that her thighs had not been registered at the Sanitation Department: they were made of Austrian flesh.

The bartender was watering the flowerpots on the windowsill. He was unaffected by the merrymaking. He knew their madness inside out, but this year they had gone beyond everything. He had already ejected the waitress a number of times, but in the end, after the musicians threatened to boycott the bar, he gave in. Business was not too good this year. There was competition from the pastry shop: those irresistible strawberry tarts.

After her dance the waitress imitated the twins, played an imaginary violin like Mandelbaum, made herself small like the yanuka. Everyone was hilarious. Pappenheim said that he anticipated a wonderful season. A number of artists had let him down, of course, failed to reply to his telegrams—no doubt it was all because of the bureaucratic disorder.

"And if we have to emigrate?" asked Sally.

"Then we'll emigrate," said Pappenheim. "There are wonderful places in Poland."

The smell of the bar worked wonders on Dr. Pappenheim's mood. His worries left him. The waitress was irrepressible. She told jokes, cursed the Austrian cabbage, and swore an oath of loyalty to Dr. Pappenheim's Jewish Order.

Suddenly a silence fell on the bar, a silence mingled with darkness. The words lay crushed. Dr. Pappenheim took off his straw cap. It seemed that he was about to introduce a famous new artist.

"What shall we order?" asked Sally.

"Something strong," said Gertie without consulting Dr. Pappenheim.

Suddenly the waitress stood up, took off her stockings, and announced that all the guzzlers and gluttons were hereby invited to feast themselves on this Austrian meat. She was blind drunk. They tried to take her down to the cellar, but the bartender refused on the grounds that it was full of bottles.

"Isn't my meat tasty?" She made a beeline for Pappenheim.

"Certainly," he said.

"So why don't you take this knife and cut yourself a slice?"

"Do I look like a butcher?"

Sally said: "What do you want of him? Do you really think he's capable of it?"

"In that case, I'll cut it myself," she said and started sawing at her thigh.

There was an uproar. They ran to fetch Martin. Blood splashed onto the floor. "You won't leave me here," she screamed. "I'm coming too!" The clumsy musicians stood there helplessly. The terror curdled in their eyes.

Then Pappenheim stood up and said: "What did you imagine? Wherever we go you will go too." But she was beyond hearing.

After Martin had dressed her wound they took her up to the lobby and wrapped her in a green woolen blanket. A shiver passed through the hotel: despair had driven her out of her mind.

The next day the hotel was sunk in a frozen silence. The waitress slept, and gray shadows hovered over her sleep. The musicians huddled together on the lawn like a frightened herd. The church tower cast a long shadow over the Imperial Gardens. Shutz did not stir from the schoolgirl's side. He was now afraid of her clear-eyed gaze. Her eyes seemed to absorb everything. Shutz told her that the waitress, the half-Jewess, was a very nice woman, but it was a pity that some kind of restlessness seemed to be disturbing her peace of mind.

"And the wound?" she asked abruptly. Shutz tried to play the whole thing down and said that despite everything the wound was very superficial.

Karl sat in an armchair and looked at the illuminated aquarium. The headwaiter approached and told him about the terrible catastrophe that had taken place in the aquarium the year before. A nature lover had brought some blue Cambium fishes and persuaded the hotel owner to put them in with the other fish. The hotel owner was a little apprehensive about these blue fish, but in the end he agreed. For the first few days the blue Cambium fish disported themselves gaily in the water, but one night they suddenly fell on the other fish and massacred them horribly. In the morning the floor of the aquarium was full of corpses.

"And are these the descendants of the murderers?" asked Karl.

"No. The hotel owner sentenced the murderers to death."

"So these are other fishes then?"

"Yes, new ones. I'm very fond of them. Look how grandly they sweep through the water. There's something magnificent about them, don't you think?"

"Do they live in peace among themselves?" asked Karl.

"I think so," said the headwaiter. "The green ones are very modest and retiring, not at all belligerent."

"Don't you think they should be separated?"

"Perhaps they should," said the headwaiter.

15

Tranquil, temperate nights returned to Badenheim. They wrapped the yanuka in two blankets and seated him on the verandah. The hotel guests looked after him like an adopted child. From time to time an express letter found its way into the town and caused a small commotion: some deal that had not gone through. A traveling salesman who had not heard about the restrictions arrived on a business trip. He could not understand: in the villages everything was quiet. What was going on?

"So it's back to Poland!" he laughed. "And I once ran away from there!"

"We all lived in Poland once, and we're all going back there," said Pappenheim.

"What's the point in going back there now? I represent a well-known firm. The idea of going back there now doesn't appeal to me in the least."

If it hadn't been for these distant greetings from the outside world, it would probably have been easier to get used to the isolation. But the occasional stray letter that found its way through disturbed the quiet and stirred up a momentary commotion.

"What do they write?"

"I've already learned to do without letters and newspapers."

"And I, unfortunately, have not learned to do without them," said Dr. Pappenheim.

Letters and newspapers. The rustle of paper was no longer heard in the hotel. The silence was dense, and from day to day it grew denser.

"I'm not worried," the traveling salesman said, recovering his spirits. "Everything's at the firm's expense, let them worry. I've kept my part of the bargain. They can foot the bill for anything that goes wrong. They've exploited me enough all these years. Let them pay my expenses now."

"You're a lucky fellow to have landed up here on your business travels."

"Once years ago I was trapped in a country village by a spring snowfall. For a whole month I slept there. And all at the firm's expense."

"You won't go to Poland though?"

"If they're prepared to foot the bill for such a long journey I don't mind going."

The next day the salesman put on a white suit and seated himself at the entrance to the pastry shop. He was like a soldier taught by long years of army service to get the most out of every opportunity for rest that came his way. At the end of the week he would get the sentries at the gate to sign for him. It wasn't his fault that he had been held up here.

Since one day ran into the next and the sentries at

the gate informed him that there was no intention at present of opening it to free traffic, he came to the conclusion that there was no point in living like a thief in the back quarters of the hotel, and he took himself a proper room, as befitting the representative of a well-known firm. The other guests were as delighted with him as if he were a messenger bringing glad tidings from afar. He dressed with great care and announced loudly from time to time: "Salo will now take a rest at the firm's expense. A rest at the firm's expense is worth its weight in gold." Afterwards he would go for a walk in the gardens, that too at the expense of the firm. Whatever he did now was strictly in accordance with company regulations. The firm required him to rest so that he would be healthy, and so that when the time came he would retire healthy too.

Finally the letters stopped altogether. The musicians sat conferring together in low voices: what about next season?

"Rehearsals, children, rehearsals," urged Pappenheim. "Soon we'll be on our way to Poland and you're not rehearsing? Artistic standards in Poland are high."

The next day Dr. Pappenheim informed them that they had been promoted, and from now on he would pay them according to the highest scale for musicians. They were very pleased. The conductor took the opportunity to reprove them for their laziness and said that the impresario's generosity was extraordinary. He himself would not have promoted them. Everyone was suddenly behaving with strange generosity. The headwaiter would often appear in the dining room and ask the guests if they were satisfied with the food. Apparently it was the hotel owner who had sent him—or perhaps he himself felt that it was part of his duty.

"Isn't it nice here?" asked Karl.

"Very nice," said Lotte.

"It takes a little time to get used to the local pleasures."

Karl never stopped talking about his two sons who had been imprisoned in a barracks by the General. "They must be exercising now," he would say. "They must be running."

16

The days slipped by. A cold light broke out of the north and spread through the long corridor. It seemed not like light but needles cutting the carpet into squares. The people hugged the walls like shadows.

The schoolgirl had grown very tall. Her tight-fitting leather jacket suited her slender figure but her cheeks, her pampered pink cheeks, had lost their bloom. Dr. Shutz tried to wrap her in his own coat, but she would not let him.

A laugh like the breaking of delicate glass was heard in the lobby. "Aren't we going to see you anymore?" asked a high-pitched woman's voice. There was no reply, and for a moment it seemed as if the voice were questioning itself.

The schoolgirl stood up and said, "Come, Shutzi, let's go out. What are we sitting here for?" There was a strange assertiveness in her voice which did not suit her delicate, fragile appearance at all.

"In a little while they'll serve ice cream," said Shutz, in an attempt to curb her impulsiveness. She sat down again and looked sharply around her with her big green eyes, as if she wanted to silence the whispering voices with her looks.

They had been sitting there for hours. The fading light caught the bush of yellow broom growing next to the window. The lobby darkened, and there was a moment of relief.

The people exchanged glances. The schoolgirl did not take her hands from her knees. Her fingers now looked somewhat transparent, and longer than usual.

"Ice cream will soon be served," announced the baritone voice of the headwaiter. Even before the announcement was over he and his retinue were standing in the doorway like puppets on a stage. For a moment they stood there, showing off the dish in all its splendor before it was devoured: pineapples and ice cream.

"There, what did I tell you?" said Shutz, in the tone of a father speaking to his adolescent daughter. The schoolgirl raised her eyes and gave him a cold, reproving look.

The people ate silently, absorbed in their little pleasure. Flakes of darkness now filled the corners of the room, and the space grew more confined. Karl and Lotte sat secluded in a corner.

"The fish in the aquarium, what's happened to the fish in the aquarium?" Karl suddenly whispered.

"Nothing, they're swimming as usual."

"I mean the green ones; where have the green ones disappeared to?"

"How strange," she said. "You watch them all the time."

Karl took the little dish and raised it to his lips, but before tasting the ice cream he said, "The green ones, the prettiest fish in the aquarium, have disappeared without anyone even noticing." He tasted the ice cream and carefully replaced the dish on the low table.

The coffee soon arrived—rich, aromatic coffee. Frau Zauberblit remarked, "The headwaiter is plying us with delicacies and we'll have to thank him for it for the rest of our lives."

"He's trying to deny us the pleasures of the world to come," said Samitzky.

"How do you mean?"

"This isn't coffee, it's myrrh."

The headwaiter apologized, saying it was Brazilian coffee from the stocks.

Darkness fell. The glowing fireplace illuminated the people sitting around it and the silent, familiar music settled on the room again. The schoolgirl was absorbed in her own reflections. Shutz lit his pipe, crossed his legs, and sat back as if he had surrendered himself to the soft hands of the twilight; and while they were all sitting there in the silence Dr. Langmann appeared, leaning on his stick.

He stood in the doorway and announced: "I went to the Department, to see the director, and demanded a re-examination."

"A re-examination of what?" Shutz opened his eyes.

"Of my case, my specific case."

"And how can we help you?"

"I'm not asking for help."

It was, of course, a delayed anger that was oppressing him, seeking an outlet. He stood in the doorway waiting for someone to start an argument, but the people weren't angry with him. "My opinion, in any case, is the same as ever," he declared.

"And what is your opinion?"

"I am an Austrian born and bred, and the laws of Austria apply to me as long as I live."

"But you also happen to be a Jew, if I'm not mistaken."

"A Jew. What does that mean? Perhaps you would be so kind as to tell me what it means?"

"As far as we're concerned," said Frau Zauberblit, "you can renounce the connection any time you like."

"That is my argument precisely."

"So why are you angry with us?"

"But Pappenheim, what about Pappenheim? Haven't you heard him calling us the Order of Jewish Nobility?"

"I never knew," said Shutz, "that Dr. Pappenheim had such a developed sense of humor."

"Such declarations should not be taken lightly," said Dr. Langmann sternly.

Shutz went out to fetch some coals to feed the fire. The schoolgirl's face changed color. Shutz did not approach her. He concentrated his gaze more and more on the sparks flying from the fire. A strange intimacy descended on the dark lobby, an intimacy without words. Dr. Langmann lit his pipe and the tobacco smoke spread its sweet aroma.

Suddenly, the schoolgirl stood up and said: "Why don't you take me out of here? Can't you see that I can't stand it any longer?" Shutz rose and stood panic-stricken by her side, but even as he held out his hand she fell to the ground in a faint.

"The child is unwell," cried Frau Zauberblit. "Bring some brandy."

Thus the twilight hour was shattered. Shutz knelt down and lifted her onto the sofa. The people stood around her looking chastised, as if the facts of life had suddenly given them a slap in the face.

The secret was out. The schoolgirl was three months pregnant. Dr. Shutz was embarrassed and confused. He sat down to write a long letter to his mother, informing her that an important change had taken place in his life. He was about to be married to a fine woman; he was sure that she would be pleased by his choice. For the moment, however, he had been left without a penny to his name. If she could send him some money by express or special delivery he would be very grateful. He folded the letter and put it in an envelope, but on the way to post it he remembered that everything was shut, including the Post Office.

17

Trude's hallucinations disappeared. Once again she stood by the open window. Martin watered the garden and painted the back entrance. The neglected back entrance had been a weight on his mind ever since the inspector's visit. He had already registered himself and Trude. The procedure was brief.

"Jew?"

"Jew."

"Jewess?"

"Jewess."

"And Helena?" asked the clerk.

"She is no longer a Jewess," smiled Martin.

The clerk asked many questions, especially about Helena. Martin was confused and did not know how to reply: when he returned and told Trude she looked at him with eyes full of affection, as if he had brought her a message from a different world. She was now given over entirely to the memories of her childhood. A number of Polish words surfaced in her memory, and whenever they came back to her she smiled. Helena did not write. Very few letters arrived, and the ones that did only brought disruption in their wake. The people who were accustomed to swimming in the pool now stood on the tennis court. The conductor spent a lot of time doing exercises.

Trude no longer said, "How transparent they are, how thin." She spoke of her childhood in Poland. She had run away from home on a silly impulse. Her parents had never forgiven her. For years she had not spoken of it.

When she began to speak at last Martin said, "You're still living there in the mountains." Now he sat and wondered: there was a melody in her voice, as if some distant music was animating her face.

Trude also said: "If God wills it, a person returns to the land of his birth."

"Will they forgive me?" This question now came up regularly, between one meal and the next. Then Trude would go back to the window or leaf through a magazine. And once she even said, "Helena will come back. I'm sure that she'll come back."

Professor Fussholdt read the proofs of his book. At one time his lectures had given rise to quite a controversy in academic circles. It was he who had called Theodore Herzl "a hack writer with messianic pretensions," and his associates "petty functionaries who jumped on the golden bandwagon." Martin Buber too did not escape his barbs. It was Fussholdt who had said that Buber couldn't make up his mind if he was a prophet or a professor. If anyone deserved the title of a great Jew, according to

Fussholdt, it was Karl Kraus: he had revived satire. And now the professor was sitting and proofreading his latest book. Who was he attacking now? The journalists, the hacks, so-called "Jewish art?" Perhaps his book was about Hans Herzl, Theodore's son who had converted to Christianity. Or perhaps it was a book about satire, the only art form appropriate to our lives.

Frau Zauberblit sat in her room. The thermometer read 101.2, and the threads of blood in her phlegm were as thick as worms. The pains grew worse and shifted from rib to rib. To die sane and never to return to the sanitorium—this was her firm resolution. Death had ceased to preoccupy her. She now believed, quite simply and literally, in the world to come.

She loved the flowers in the Luxembourg Gardens, the short walks, everything called "Badenheim": the looks and the words. Samitzky drank steadily. He spoke German mixed with Polish, and told stories about the town of his birth all the time.

The night before, Frau Zauberblit had written an outline of her will:

1) Jewelry—to the yanuka, for his musical education;
2) Cash—to the twins;
3) Clothes—to Sally and Gertie;
4) Household effects—to the headwaiter;
5) Her body was not to be cremated. Dr. Pappenheim was to say Kaddish.

She put the piece of paper away in a drawer. Her temperature climbed slowly. The habit of writing down every fluctuation in her temperature, a habit to which she had grown accustomed in the sanitorium and which she detested, was now a secret she shared only with herself. She would write it down and laugh, as if she were laughing at herself for a silly habit she could not shed.

She wrote a lot of letters. She remembered her old nurse and sent her money, but above all it was Samitzky and his sick melody that she loved. It was as if their friendship were not a matter of days but of years without number. Many of the old regulars had not come this year. She felt affection for them all, even Mitzi.

"If Mandelbaum lets us down we'll invite Kraus, at my expense—only don't be sad, Dr. Pappenheim, don't be sad." Samitzky drank and she did not tell him to stop. She loved him and his drunkenness.

18

The light stood still. There was a frozen kind of attentiveness in the air. An alien orange shadow gnawed stealthily at the geranium leaves. The creepers absorbed the bitter, furtive damp. Pappenheim spoiled the musicians and bought them chocolates and cream cakes. The musicians were submissive, full of gratitude. The quarrels were over. And the strange new light filtered through the clouds and illuminated the broad verandah. Dr. Shutz's love was no longer lighthearted as in days gone by. The orange shadow now lay on him and his beloved. The schoolgirl huddled into his summer coat as if afraid of a sudden separation.

The Post Office was locked. Cold lights caressed the smooth marble steps. The portals with their gothic carvings were somehow reminiscent of a ruined monument. The night before Dr. Pappenheim stood next to the closed Post Office and laughed. "Everything's been shut down."

While Dr. Pappenheim was standing next to the Post Office a desperate struggle was going on in the pharmacy. Two strangers had forced their way in and were looting the "toxica" cupboard. Martin fought them off, took the vials away from them and shouted, "I won't allow it!" They were two haggard men who had arrived a few days before. On their faces was an icy despair.

Mandelbaum and his trio arrived like thieves in the night. Pappenheim took them down to the ground floor and gave them tea.

"What happened?"

"We received a transfer," said Mandelbaum.

"Did you ask for it?"

"Of course we did. A young man, a junior officer, has already transferred our papers. We explained that we had to get to the Festival. He laughed and gave his permission. What do you say, we're in for it, eh?"

"It's wonderful," said Pappenheim. "I thought you'd never make it. You must rest now."

The net had caught up with them in the holiday town of Reizenbach. At first the whole thing seemed like a joke, but it soon became clear that the Austrians were no less efficient than the Germans. The locals were sent home and the Jews—yes sir, plain and simple and without any beating about the bush—the Jews were put into quarantine! Mandelbaum had sent letters to the Academy but there was no reply. But for that young officer he would never have escaped. "A little enterprise. The Jews have always been famous for their enterprise, isn't that so, Dr. Pappenheim?" joked Mandelbaum.

Dr. Pappenheim ran joyfully to fetch the head-waiter. The headwaiter came and stood there over-come with awe, as if it was the Emperor Franz Josef himself he had been called upon to serve.

For years Dr. Pappenheim had been trying to entice Mandelbaum to Badenheim. But year fol-lowed year and he never arrived. Pappenheim often boasted of his promises, seeing them as signs of affection and of hope for the future—and last year he had actually succeeded in breaching the wall and had been received in the great man's office in the Academy. And Mandelbaum had promised him that this summer he would come. Dr. Pappenheim had not been able to believe his ears. And now the great artist was finally here. It was doubtful if he had really wanted to come. But in any case he was here now, there was no denying the fact that he was here.

"Are we all Jews here?" inquired Mandelbaum lightly, as if he weren't the great Mandelbaum at all.

"The servants ran away, but the headwaiter him-self is a Jew born and bred, thank God, and one other waitress too."

"So everything is kosher then," the great man joked.

The headwaiter allowed himself to say, "Here in Badenheim the maestro has many admirers."

Later they went on a comprehensive tour. Man-delbaum expressed his admiration. He said that Badenheim was far more beautiful than Reizenbach. If he had known he would have come long ago. A man never knew where true beauty lay hidden or where his true admirers were. After the tour they sat in the lounge and Mandelbaum suddenly laughed out loud: "The Academy doesn't answer my letters!

You hear, the Academy ignores its President, it denies its Founder! Isn't that food for thought?"

"They'll be sorry one day," said Dr. Pappenheim. He sat and explained: "The guests here are an extremely pleasant lot. And this year, due to the restrictions, the atmosphere is intimate. If the maestro agrees to appear, it will be the experience of our lives."

"Me? I'm just a Jew, a number, a file. If not for the junior officer I would still be rotting in Reizenbach. What do you need me for? Am I a rabbi, a cantor?"

"You are our maestro, our one and only maestro and the only one we want."

Mandelbaum turned to his trio and said: "We'll play for you like a band of Jewish minstrels. The Academy refuses to reply to its President, it ignores registered letters, it ignores express letters. We'll be your Jewish minstrels."

The heavy, clumsy musicians stood to one side and did not open their mouths. The great artist inspired them with awe. They sat huddled together like tame birds, following his every move. The conductor too watched him as if hypnotized. The Princess Milbaum, who knew all the famous artists in Vienna and had heard the news of his arrival, descended from her royal throne and said: "Professor Mandelbaum! So Professor Mandelbaum too is amongst us!"

Mandelbaum rose and kissed her hand. He said, "At last my disgrace has been exposed in public."

"And what does the Royal Academy have to say?"

"They ignore my letters."

"I would break off all connection with them, once

and for all. That would teach them a lesson, that would teach them some manners."

Dr. Pappenheim felt uneasy, as if greater powers than he had intervened.

Mandelbaum told her about Reizenbach. The Princess listened to the grotesque tale and said: "They'll pay for it." Proud lightning flashed from her eyes.

"And here?" Mandelbaum inquired.

"Rotten to the core," she declared.

That very night Mandelbaum shut himself up in his room; the clean, polished notes cut through the silence. Now a new fear fell on the people: Mandelbaum.

19

The leaden sun hung heavily over the cold horizon.

"How far is it from here to Vienna?" someone asked aimlessly.

"About two hundred kilometers, I should imagine, or even less." The words floated in the void like tired, dispirited birds. Downstairs, in the kitchen, they were making the beloved apple strudel. The sweet smell wafted over the verandah.

"Why shouldn't we go and apply for a visa?" said one of the musicians, who had been a bit of a wanderer in his youth.

"And if you had a visa, where would you go?" The man fell silent, as if he had been asked an embarrassing question.

The conductor put down his cards and said, "For my part, I'm ready to go anywhere."

Martin took out the winter clothes and the smell of mothballs spread through the house. The dream of Poland had quieted Trude. Martin would sit by her side and promise that everything would be all right. "We came from Poland and now we have to go back to Poland. Whoever was born there has to go back there," he would repeat in a kind of sing-song.

A group of angry people stood by the telephone and cursed the bureaucracy that had suddenly, without any advance warning, cut them off from their loved ones. "Order!" they cried bitterly. "Order!" A few even bestirred themselves to write long, detailed letters complaining of all the inconvenience that had been caused them by the disconnection. They demanded compensation from travel agencies, from the authorities who were detaining them here. All these complaints were, of course, in vain. The lines had all been cut, the Post Office was shut. The maids had flown as if the houses were on fire. The town had begun to live its life inside itself.

"What will they do with us there in Poland?" asked one of the musicians.

"What do you mean? You'll be a musician, just as you've always been," said the friend sitting half asleep next to him.

"In that case why send us there at all?"

The friend sought an impressive formula. "Historical necessity," he said.

"Kill me, I don't understand it. Ordinary common sense can't comprehend it."

"In that case, kill your ordinary common sense and maybe you'll begin to understand."

The houses slowly filled with silence. The straggly

creepers grew wild. The acacias bloomed without stopping. Autumn and spring mingled strangely. At night there was no air to breathe. Samitzky was drinking heavily. He drank like a peasant, and spoke a mixture of Polish and Yiddish. Of all the languages he knew it seemed that the only one that remained was this language of his youth.

"Why do you drink so much, my dear?" asked Frau Zauberblit gently.

"When a man goes home he should be happy."

"It's cold there, really cold."

"Yes, but it's a healthy cold, a clear cold, a cold with hope for the future."

The registration was over. The officials now sat in the Sanitation Department drinking tea. They had done what they had been told to do. Now they were waiting for instructions.

But in the streets there were still surprises. A few days before a man had stood next to the Post Office, a citizen of Badenheim and a major in the First World War, and asked, in the tone which he had no doubt been accustomed to using in the army, why the Post Office was closed. And Dr. Pappenheim, who could not rid himself of the habit of visiting the closed Post Office every day, replied, perhaps incautiously, that the town was in quarantine.

"I don't understand," said the major. "Is there an epidemic?"

"A Jewish epidemic."

"Is that supposed to be a joke?"

"It's no joking matter—try to leave and see."

The man turned his head and his narrow, steely look, the look of a man used to scanning maps and open expanses, focused on the short figure of Dr.

Pappenheim as if he were about to reprimand him or dismiss him from his presence.

"Is the major not yet registered with the Sanitation Department?" Dr. Pappenheim continued, in a provocative tone of voice.

For two days the major fought the Sanitation Department. He cursed the Jews and the bureaucracy and terrorized the deserted streets of the town. In the end he shot himself in the head. Dr. Langmann, who did not stir from his place at the window, remarked to himself: "You must admit that the Jews are an ugly people. I can't see that they're any use to anyone."

The conductor put down his cards and said, "Do you remember anything from home?"

"What home?" said the musician Blumenthal, a naïve man who seemed to go through life in a kind of daze. At the beginning, in the early days of the band, the conductor had treated him harshly and mocked him. But nothing had helped. He had remained as dreamy as ever.

"Your Jewish home."

"Nothing."

"My parents," said the conductor, "converted to Christianity, damn it all."

"In that case, why don't you leave everything here and go back to Vienna?"

"My dear friend, my name appears in a place of honor on the lists of the Sanitation Department."

"What do they want of us?"

"It's hard to understand," said the conductor, as if he had been given a complicated score to read. "If the rumor that we're being transferred to Poland is right, we'll have to start studying. I don't know anything."

"At our age we're a little past it already, aren't we?"

"There's no help for it. We'll have to learn Polish."

"Do you really think so?"

20

The following days were quiet. The pastry shop was closed down, and the creepers grew untrammeled over the green shutters. In the bar they stopped serving drinks. The fish in the aquarium flourished and grew fat. If it hadn't been for the pungent smell of tobacco lingering in the air, the bar would have resembled a modest debating club.

Dr. Pappenheim decided to put his papers in order and tore up one after the other: files, old letters, contracts, advertisements, and all kinds of other papers that filled the room to overflowing. After he had finished clearing everything out he went for a walk with Sally and Gertie. Sally was wearing a lace dress which the old Graf had brought her from Venice and Gertie was wearing something short.

"Let's go out," said Dr. Pappenheim. "I've already done my work for today."

At the entrance to the pastry shop stood the old

pastry cook wearing a blue suit. After the years he had spent with the pastry shop owner he had no will of his own left. A dumb helplessness stared from his long face.

"Getting ready, are we?" asked Dr. Pappenheim.

At this question the old man approached them and said, "I'm ready."

"There's no hurry, there's still time."

"I wanted to ask the doctor," said the pastry cook very respectfully, "how the transfer will take place?"

"By train. Train journeys are nice, aren't they?"

The long years in the confined bakery had not bowed the old man's peasant's body. He looked like a peasant who had married his daughters off long ago and had nothing left now but leisure and memories.

"May I be permitted to ask a personal question?" said the pastry cook. "I've been working here for thirty years on end. Will my pension be recognized there too?"

"Everything will be transferred there," said Dr. Pappenheim. "No one will be deprived."

"That's what I thought," said the pastry cook.

They walked on. The chestnut trees were shedding their leaves. A gaping emptiness stared mutely from the square. All these years in Badenheim. Never a moment to himself. A slave to the caprices of the artists. Pappenheim now felt for the first time that his time was his own. "I would like to go back to research," he suddenly said without any connection to anything.

"And what will we do?" said Sally. "What would you suggest, Dr. Pappenheim? I imagine that in the evenings we might be able to attend a course of lectures. What's your opinion? All large cities have lecture courses in the evenings. In Vienna I remember there used to be advertisements about evening courses."

"Of course," said Dr. Pappenheim.

In Princess Salpina's garden the roses grew riotously, as if they were being fed on rotten beets. The house stood empty. At the gate, the wooden gate, there was no barking dog. In recent years the Princess had not taken part in the busy life of Badenheim, preferring to live in Vienna. And the neat little house had lost its glory, but not its secret. At first she too had been enthusiastic about the twins, but one evening, without any apparent reason, she had abandoned Badenheim. Later on she had written a long letter, full of anger, in which she set forth all her complaints against the twins. Dr. Pappenheim had replied and defended their honor.

"Why is she angry with us?" asked Sally.

"I don't know. If only I did," said Pappenheim, shrugging his shoulders.

"We could have left together. Wouldn't it have been nice if we could all have left together?"

"Princess Salpina is very fond of Slavic art. She studied it in Berlin," said Gertie, and immediately fell silent in embarrassment at having produced this remark.

"Her knowledge of Slavic art is, indeed, very thorough," said Dr. Pappenheim.

"Couldn't we write to her?"

"I wrote her a long letter," said Dr. Pappenheim, "but she never replied."

They walked for a long time. Pappenheim was in a good mood and he told them about his student days in Dresden. Dresden was a pretty town but Vienna was even better. It was hard for anyone born in

Vienna to live anywhere else. When they returned to the hotel they found the yanuka crying "I want to go home."

Sally bought him a pink box of candy, but the child would not stop crying. When she saw that the sweets had not helped, Gertie stood up and announced: "I'm going to buy you an electric train with real rails."

The child calmed down. Gertie sat with him and told him that Warsaw was a big city with lots of toy stores. As soon as they arrived in Warsaw, she would buy him an electric train. The boy asked a lot of questions and Gertie answered at length: Warsaw was the capital of Poland and it had everything that anyone could possibly want.

21

Once more a few stray letters filtered through, raising a forgotten world from oblivion. One of Mitzi's old lovers sent her a picture postcard with a complimentary message. Mitzi cried. Salo stood by her side and consoled her, saying that one shouldn't attach too much importance to the written word, but his consolations were of no avail. She cried like a little girl.

The conductor received his bank statement. He shut himself up in his room and studied it. His shares had gone up.

Karl too received a letter, from his oldest son. The boy wrote at length, with much sensitivity, of his experiences at his new school, the military academy. He had registered, passed the entrance exams, and now he was taking his first steps in the new school. As far as his studies were concerned he had already obtained two high marks, and in the practical training too he was making progress. He ate a lot of cabbage and sausages, drank beer, did exercises. Soon they would be going on their first forced march. They boy had an athletic build and he had already picked up some of the slang expressions popular in the school. He had a nickname, "Adam's Apple," and he had cleared all the hurdles in the obstacle course without a single slip. Karl showed the letter to Lotte. Lotte read it and said that the boy's style was flawless. And for a moment the father forgot his wrath. His heart filled with pride.

"He's a very sensitive boy. How can he stand all that brutality?"

"Can't you see? The boy is already capable of forming his own judgments." This sentence, which was pronounced in a calm, matter-of-fact tone, suddenly gave Karl back the faith that his beloved son was not lost to him.

Shutz did not receive a letter. The schoolgirl spent all her time lying on the verandah and soaking up the mild sun. She was absorbed in herself and the fetus inside her. Shutz tried in vain to make her talk. It seemed that everything between them had been exhausted. She loved the sun more than anything. Shutz was now outside her, the words between them fewer and fewer. Strangely enough, he seemed not to notice.

And the isolated letters gave rise to a kind of chilly despair. Only now, it seemed, did the people realize what was happening here. "The telephone, the telephone!" some cried aloud.

The pharmacy was a hive of activity. People bought drugs indiscriminately. At first Martin was pleased, until he realized what they were up to. They were building up private stocks of poisonous drugs and narcotics. He took fright and locked the door. The people begged, "Open up, open up!" When they saw that their pleading led nowhere a conspiracy of wordless looks was set afoot and in the end the pharmacy was broken into.

The people were being driven out of their minds by their longings. They stood by the gates and asked: "When will we leave? When?"

"What have you got to complain about?" said the sentry. "You don't have drill or guard duty, do you?"

They were like sick people asking about their illness. If the doctor refused to explain, maybe they could get something out of the nurse?

No more artists came. Dr. Pappenheim went to the gate every day. As long as the ensemble was not complete there would be no redemption. We complement one another, and as long as one of us is missing we will not be saved—this was the source of his despair.

At the very moment when despair had almost taken over, Frau Zauberblit stood up and announced that that evening the twins would perform.

The twins had grown taller and looked like two emaciated boys, athletes or dancers. The moment they ascended the stage their emaciation took on a compelling power. Their mastery was such that the words did not seem like words at all: they were as pure and abstract as if they had never been touched by human mouths.

For a whole hour they stood there on the stage in total concentration. And by the end of the hour the words did their work alone, flying through the air like birds on fire.

"They've done it, I told you they'd do it!" said Dr.

Pappenheim. There were tears in his eyes. Sally
hurried to bring lemonade. After the performance
the seriousness left the twins' faces. Now they
seemed like two boys who had just come home after
winning a race, pleased with themselves but a little
empty. They told jokes and the people laughed.
Princess Milbaum did not come down to see the
miracle. Her hostility was venomous. A few days
before she suddenly stood up and announced that
she still intended to expose a few ugly affairs. She
called Pappenheim an international criminal. Then
she shut herself up in her room and wrote long,
detailed letters about those clowns, the *Ostjuden,*
who had taken over Badenheim and were dragging
every bit of true culture through the dirt.

22

The food supplies did not arrive and the hotel owner opened up the stores. The headwaiter stood at the storeroom door and illuminated the darkness with a flashlight. His fingers trembled, as if the treasures of the world to come had suddenly been revealed to him. It was a big room full of antique furniture. The kind of silence only found in sealed-off places hung congealed in the air.

"From here?" asked the headwaiter reverentially.

"Yes," said the hotel owner, smiling as if there were nothing left to regret.

The headwaiter was as happy as if he had been promoted. The hotel was now full of the fragrant aromas of liqueurs, Swiss chocolate, French wine, pecans, and fine peach preserves. The people sat at the tables and ate with quiet enjoyment.

"This is a time we'll remember forever," exulted the musician Zimbelman.

"Don't worry, we'll have to pay for it in hard cash," said the conductor.

The twins too descended from their seclusion to taste the new delicacies. They had grown very thin. Their white coats were too wide for their narrow shoulders. How alike they were!

Sally asked: "How are the artists?"

And the headwaiter said happily, "It's good to see the artists among us."

The twins now looked like two well brought up young boys of good family. They laughed and asked for details, and the headwaiter took time off to give them a lesson in French gastronomy. He was an ardent disciple of French cooking and had been trying for years to banish the heavy Austrian smells from the hotel kitchen.

Evening fell. The yanuka sang the famous lullaby "Rozinkes mit Mandleh." Recently he had been sunk in melancholy and refused to sing. Pappenheim had spoken to him a number of times but the child would not be consoled; he was angry and sad. It was the headwaiter's finest hour. He pronounced the French names as if he were caressing the syllables with his tongue, as if he were speaking not of food but of living creatures who needed to be treated with affection.

The old, familiar expression returned to Gertie's and Sally's faces, the expression they had worn when they were elegant young women, soliciting discreetly for customers. The end of the summer was astonishingly beautiful, and from the verandah Badenheim looked like a carpet studded with golden lights. There were no new announcements on the notice board. The conductor left the musicians to their own devices. The half-Jewish waitress sat with the guests, wearing a blue dress. There was a skeptical smile on her lips. Martin had cared for her devotedly and she had recovered. The headwaiter pampered her with delicacies and warm words.

And there was a strange lull. People spent a lot of time dozing in the armchairs. Salo sat next to the conductor and said that he was enjoying his stay here very much. There was no point in trying to hurry things up. And it wouldn't break the hotel owner either. The conductor was annoyed and said that it wasn't fair of Salo. But Salo went on teasing him and said that he was really enjoying all this disorder, it was an ill wind that blew nobody any good. Prices had gone up in recent years. The firm was getting rich and he was always in debt. Here he lacked for nothing, he had shelter, music, pleasant company. What did he care? Let them put everything onto the bill. The conductor was indignant at Salo's words and tone but said nothing.

Suddenly a kind of trance seemed to take hold of the people. The headwaiter went from table to table saying, "Who knows if I'll ever be able to offer you such delicacies again?" There were tears in his eyes. But the people had lost their appetites. They sat staring at the aquarium and the oil painting on the wall next to it. The hotel owner stood silently in the doorway.

Mandelbaum bullied his trio mercilessly. He raged, threatened, and banged on the table with his fists. In the silent lobby it sounded as if something terrible was happening upstairs. Suddenly the schoolgirl said, "Someone should go upstairs and rescue them. Mandelbaum's torturing them like a sadist." But no one stood up. They all went on staring into space and nobody moved. Even the appearance of the little coffee cups did not arouse them. The schoolgirl stood up and said that she was sick and tired of the company here. Upstairs a sadist was torturing innocent people, and here everybody just went on sitting as if nothing was happening.

23

To round off the season they served golden cider, a subtle drink that always gave rise to a certain delicate melancholy. The headwaiter was proud of this drink, which was made from his own special recipe. Usually at this hour the people would have been busy packing, saying good-by to their friends, and taking a last look at Badenheim from the verandah before leaving the next morning.

This time the cider, which the headwaiter served with great deliberation, had a pungent, slightly intoxicating taste. The people sipped slowly from the rustic steins, with a strange, stealthy enjoyment.

Usually at this hour Dr. Pappenheim would sit down and sum up what he called "the lessons of the season": the irresponsible musicians, the eternal deficit, and all the troubles, big and small, that ruined his happiness. But this year all his aggravation vanished. He felt no resentment against anyone. He wanted to stand up and thank the people for their confidence, their friendship, their cooperation, to mention the artists who had failed to turn up by name and to say a few words of praise in their honor; to explain that from now on there would be no difference, either in place or time, between Badenheim and Vienna, between the local residents and summer guests. From now on it would all be Badenheim, here or in some other place, it made no difference.

While these words were galloping through Dr. Pappenheim's head, the hotel owner appeared in the doorway and said that he wanted to beg the pardon of everyone present for the irregularities—perhaps he too had something to blame himself for, and for this at any rate he begged their pardon. He spoke as calmly and quietly as if he were measuring his words with a ruler.

A momentary commotion broke out on the verandah. Frau Zauberblit rose from her place and said that on no account was the hotel owner to blame himself for anything. Every year in Badenheim was a celebration, and this year was no exception.

The headwaiter went on pouring out the cider. It was chilly on the verandah, and the people wrapped their legs in woolen blankets. The old familiar warmth settled on the verandah again. The hotel owner joined the guests. He looked a little shy. It seemed that at any moment now someone would stand up and say, as someone said every year, "Come, children—to your packing, to your packing!" But no one stood up. The moment seemed frozen in time.

The sunlight illuminated the verandah and the

faces of the people. Martin sat outside in an armchair, with Trude beside him. They sat without
speaking, as if nothing had happened. The musicians
lounged about on the lawn. At any moment now, it
seemed, the conductor would call out, "Upstairs,
boys, upstairs and get into your uniforms!" But
nobody moved. The headwaiter went on pouring the
cider into the rustic steins, which now seemed
curiously heavy, as if they were made of metal.
Shutz wrapped the schoolgirl in two extra blankets.
The sun sank gradually, leaving behind it long, cold
rays of light.

"Why won't you have a drink?" Shutz urged the
schoolgirl. "You're hurting the headwaiter's feelings. The cider is his pride and joy." The schoolgirl
sat up unwillingly and took a long gulp. Her face was
so transparent that you could see her jaws moving.

Sally and Gertie joined the party and sat next to
the yanuka. The yanuka was in a good mood and
asked their names. Pappenheim said that the yanuka
spoke no German, but he seemed to understand.
They begged him to sing: he asked them if they were
students at the university and they burst out laughing.

Even Karl was calm. He downed glass after glass,
but the cider did not make him drunk. He seemed
content: "Isn't it nice here?" he asked Lotte as he
had in the beginning.

"Very nice," said Lotte.

Darkness fell and the words died away. The
schoolgirl's face grew more and more transparent.
There was no fear or regret in her eyes. It was as if
she weren't a girl who had run away from school, but
a young woman who had known both pleasures and
disappointments in her life: she curled up in the

blankets like an experienced woman who knew the value of inanimate objects.

"What's come over the child?" The people exchanged glances. And the very same question seemed to stare from the eyes of the lover himself.

For a long time they went on looking at her. But her face gave nothing away. A sickly light seemed to shine from it. And then this light too died away and her face grew cold.

"Shall we go out for a walk this evening?" asked Shutz.

"Where to?" she said, and the words sounded less like a question than a harsh statement of fact.

24

The nights were now high and transparent. The hotel throbbed to the sounds of music. Even the laziest of musicians practiced. No one could say anymore: "Why don't you rehearse?" Never before had Badenheim heard such a concentration of sounds.

"Isn't that a feast for the ear!" exclaimed Dr. Pappenheim.

"They're driving me crazy," grumbled Mitzi.

"You wouldn't like us to appear in Poland unrehearsed, would you? What would people say?"

The summer had not smiled on Mitzi. No suitor, no friend. This one busy practicing, that one in love, that one adding up his savings. Even the dull, heavy musicians had suddenly taken it into their heads to rehearse. Fussholdt was completely absorbed in his proofreading. Mitzi wept. Her petty vanity, cultivated with so much femininity, lay in ruins around her—and without this little vanity what did she have in the world? Fussholdt again, Fussholdt and his eternal proofs. And that was all there would ever be. So what difference did it make to her if they were here or in Poland? Her tears were bitter. All the years seemed tied together in one painful knot.

"In a few days' time everything will change. We are on the threshold of a radical change," said Pappenheim, choosing his words with great deliberation.

Ten years ago Fussholdt had been a brilliant young lecturer, a friendly fellow who played ping-pong. Mitzi had not been faithful to him even then, but then his fame had made up for everything. He sunk deeper and deeper into his researches, and in Badenheim he applied himself to his books like a drunk to the bottle. Ten years with Fussholdt had left her without a spark of hope. Only an eternity of desolation.

"The idea of the journey frightens me very much," said Mitzi.

"There's nothing to be afraid of," said Dr. Pappenheim. "There are many Jews living in Poland. In the last analysis, a man has to return to his origins."

The pastry shop owner stood outside and gave vent to his indignation: "They're driving the whole town crazy. Let Pappenheim emigrate, not us. What harm have we ever done anyone? We never brought any rotten artists here, we never encouraged perversity."

"Don't you take any interest in music?" Pappenheim asked Mitzi.

She stood there like an empty vessel, and in her narrow eyes was a fear beyond hope or remedy: what was going to happen in Poland? The same thing all over again. Fussholdt with his books and Mitzi alone with herself.

"It will be completely different," said Pappenheim. "You can't imagine how different it will be."

Samitzky put his instrument down and came to stand beside them. "If only we'd practiced all these years the way we're practicing now."

"And Mandelbaum? He didn't practice, I suppose?"

"I'm not talking about great artists. But what about the rest of us? We'll roast in hell."

"The trio?" said Pappenheim. "It seems to me we have nothing to be ashamed of in that quarter. And the twins too have done fine work in recent months."

All the delicacies were finished. Strangely enough, the people weren't hungry. All they wanted were cigarettes. If only they had cigarettes they would be all right. But without cigarettes it was hell. And wonder of wonders, Sally found a packet of cigarettes. Everyone gathered round to see for themselves and Sally gave them one cigarette each. It was a high, clear night. The music wafted down from the upper floor. The people sat in the armchairs and sucked in the smoke.

"Don't they smoke?" someone asked.

"No. They used to, but Mandelbaum forbade it."

"So they overcame that too, did they?"

The headwaiter put on an impeccable black suit and sat with the guests. There was no need for formality any longer. Now he could allow himself to sit among the guests and listen to the music. Salo puffed deliberately on his cigarette. Two days had already gone by without cigarettes, and what was life without a cigarette?

"I'd give all the money owing me on my expense account for one pack of cigarettes," said Salo.

"What do you mean?" exclaimed the conductor. "It must be a fortune!"

"And my little lust, my little lust for a cigarette, is that so insignificant in your eyes?"

"Can't you control yourself?"

"I'm not a slave to the firm anymore. My little caprices are more important to me than the firm. Expense accounts won't dazzle me! But for my caprices I'd be a rich man, but I won't give them up for anyone. Let them fire me if they like!"

"Compose yourself, sir, compose yourself," said the conductor severely.

Sally told everyone: "I went through all the cupboards, there were so many bottles I could open a perfumery, but not a cigarette to be seen, and then all of a sudden in the middle of all those bottles, a whole packet full of cigarettes!"

Salo had apparently had too much to drink. He cursed the firm and all its works and swore an oath that he would never be a slave to anyone or anything again except for his own little caprices. This said, he removed all his receipts from his vest pocket and scattered them on the ground. The conductor bent down to pick them up muttering, "The man has gone quite mad."

25

Why not go outside? If not for the angry people it would have been possible to take a stroll to the square and enjoy the coolness in the air. The sun was still shining, but the angry people clung stubbornly to the old words, hoarding them like antiquated gadgets that had gone out of use. Since they were unable to liberate themselves from the old words and the fear, they prowled the streets and cast their angry shadows.

"Sport he preaches. Sport!" muttered Karl, referring to Dr. Langmann. The word *sport* had not crossed Dr. Langmann's lips, but Karl had evidently not forgotten the argument in the courtyard next to the Sanitation Department. It seemed that he would take this hostility with him wherever he went, to whatever place of exile.

Old arguments and forgotten conversations and

slips of the tongue—nothing seemed to disappear. They were all still there, clear as the day they were uttered. People avoided one another like enemies. The square stood empty and desolate.

The major's brother put on his dead brother's uniform and prowled the main street. When he came close to the hotel entrance he shouted: "Come out for inspection! I'm counting up to ten. Sergeant, take them to the parade ground. Two hours of drill, and then the obstacle course. There's a CO's inspection this week."

Salo teased him: "But officer, the men are at the front."

"Stand to attention, you cheeky fellow, stand to attention!"

"Officer," said Salo, "we've got sick call. We've been excused from morning inspection."

"Morning inspection takes first priority."

"So we're not excused then? Just a minute, I'll go and tell the men that they're not excused."

"I'm counting to ten."

"Count slowly, sir."

Karl tried to free himself from Lotte's gentle grasp. She pleaded with him: "Leave him alone, Karl, please. Can't you see that he's not really serious? He's insane."

One evening the sentries came from the gate and arrested the major's brother. He shouted and threatened, but all the old honors could not help him now. The sentries pushed him roughly. He walked off holding himself very erect, like a soldier.

Heavy, dense nights descended on Badenheim. The word *sport* was taboo. Karl stood at the doors eavesdropping. Dr. Langmann had shut himself up in his room, afraid of Karl's stares. In the circle of his stares there burned a sapphire flame.

Hard lights, lights without the soft blue of the sky, climbed the heavy bars of the windows. Words without bodies floated in the lobby.

"Are you coming?"

"In a minute, I'm coming."

"Take your coat, I'll wait outside."

The words did not seem to belong to the present. They were the words of the spring which had somehow lingered on, suspended in the void. "The program? Have you got the Festival program?" asked a woman's voice, but when she encountered Karl's angry glare she beat a hasty retreat, and the silence, the loaded silence that kept the people apart, descended on the lobby again.

"If only the front verandah could be opened . . . couldn't we get the front verandah opened?" The front verandah was overgrown with creepers. The geraniums flourished like weeds. It was dark in the daytime and no sound penetrated.

"Let's go out," said Lotte.

"And what about the fish? The fish in the aquarium—shall we abandon them to their fate?"

"No, God forbid," said Lotte.

"We're not Junkers, and we're not Prussians. We feel sorry for the little fish in the aquarium. As long as we live we'll feel sorry for the little fish in the aquarium."

"Of course we will," said Lotte.

"In that case, how can you suggest going out?"

The musicians too were afraid to leave their rooms. Karl was terrorizing everyone. Only Lotte was not afraid of him. She spoke to him softly and gently and gathered crumbs in the kitchen for the fish in the aquarium. At night Karl illuminated the water with a flashlight.

Trude's madness was now quiet and powerful. The fear had left her. She slept peacefully and her voice was calm.

"Soon we'll go to Poland and all will be well."

"And Helena will come back to us too."

"Of course."

Martin asked his wife about Poland as if she were an oracle. Ever since the pharmacy had been looted his world had collapsed. He sat in the room and never went out. Trude sometimes said, "Why don't you go out? Aren't you interested in the outside world anymore?" When she spoke about Poland her eyes lit up, and the sorrow was erased from her brow. A new, young skin seemed to be growing over her face. She laughed.

Martin asked many questions. "Are the rivers in Poland beautiful?"

And Trude spared no details. There was no country as beautiful as Poland, no air as pure as Polish air.

"And Yiddish? You know I don't speak Yiddish."

"There's nothing easier than learning Yiddish. It's a simple, beautiful language, and Polish too is a beautiful language."

There was strength in her voice and strength in her eyes. Martin stood feebly at her side. He had absorbed her sickness, but in him it was without power, without roots. Sadness gripped him like a vise. Trude berated him and said: "If you had any faith, you would be happy."

And when evening fell and the air grew dusky, she

drew the busy streets of Lodz into the room, and her mother, and her brothers and sisters; she spoke Yiddish and Polish alternately. Martin sat and listened to the many voices. And when the voices had exhausted her she said goodnight as if she were parting from people who were about to fall asleep.

26

The town was full of strangers. The shadows of the forest returned to the town and spread themselves over the paving stones of the Imperial Square. Mountain breezes blew in the alleys and there was a smell of moss. Sally and Gertie stood at their gate and offered the strangers mugs of soup.

"What is this place?" someone asked, as if waking from a troubled sleep.

"The holiday resort of Badenheim, the Music Festival city."

"Where do the concerts take place?"

"In the hall."

At the sound of these words the man seemed to come alive again.

In the late afternoon the people would gather next to the hotel entrance and Dr. Pappenheim would speak to them. How his face had changed over the past few months! He would tell them about Poland.

About the wonderful world to which they were going. "Here we have no life left," he would say. "Here everything has become empty."

Only a few days before, they had been sitting in their warm houses, busy with their flourishing practices. Now they were sitting here, without shelter. Everything had been taken from them; it was like a bad dream. Someone asked for details about housing conditions, employment, transferring foreign currency, and a man who had lost his wife on the way asked if she had perhaps gone on ahead and was already in Poland.

"Will we have a chance to hear the twins?" someone asked in the dissolving darkness.

Salo was happy. His stay here would cost the company a fortune. Everything was at their expense, even the journey to Poland. The musicians liked him and called him "the agent." And Salo, used to words and soliciting for trade, sat in the armchair and held forth: a man should broaden his horizons. Ever since he was a boy he had loved traveling. "You should make Dr. Pappenheim sign Form 101. He's sure to have it, every employer does. Travel by all means, but like me, at the company's expense."

"Form 101, what's that? I've never heard of it," said one of the musicians.

"I've been using it for years, it's an official form. I discovered it immediately. It's brought me a good bit of indirect income, I can tell you."

One of the strangers invaded the hotel and threatened to murder the owner. "*Ostjuden*, you're to blame!"

"I'm not to blame for anything." The hotel owner stood next to the stranger like a prisoner.

The man shouted and waved his fists, and since he

was in the grip of madness people approached him and tried to explain that things weren't as bad as they looked. A board of appeals would surely exempt him.

Every committee had a board of appeals, that was a well-known fact. No committee could simply do as it pleased. There was a question of procedure, after all. And if the lower courts made a mistake, then the higher courts were always there to remedy it. There was no need to get upset.

"If you're right, where does the board of appeals sit?" asked the man, a little appeased.

"They'll probably make an announcement soon."

"I don't understand," said the man. "Am I a criminal to be thrown out of my house? You tell me, please."

"It's not a question of crime, but of a misunderstanding. We too, to a certain extent, are the victims of a misunderstanding."

The words *procedure* and *appeal* seemed to satisfy him. He had apparently once studied law. He calmed down a little. The contact with the old words restored him to his sanity.

Since the hotel owner saw that the old words had a good effect on the agitated soul of the stranger, he continued to use the same tone with him. The board of appeals would surely start hearing the appeals soon. They would be sure to discover plenty of flaws in these hasty procedures. Someone had probably made a mistake. There were empty beds upstairs. He could rest a little. Tomorrow they would probably know more.

The man was embarrassed, ashamed. "I didn't know," he said. "I'm sorry. Suddenly everything was taken away from me. They drove me here on the grounds that I'm a Jew. They must have meant the *Ostjuden*. And I'm like you, an Austrian. My forefathers? I don't know. Maybe, who knows. What does it matter who my forefathers were."

Then he turned to the hotel owner and said loudly: "Please accept my apologies." The latter hurried to assist him as if he were an honored guest. They went upstairs.

"Why don't you sleep? You've been through a hard time," said the hotel owner. "Here are some pajamas, a towel."

The stranger, chastened, took off his sweater and shoes and said—as he was perhaps accustomed to saying to his wife—"Please wake me early in the morning."

27

Gray days settled on the town. In the hotel
they stopped serving meals. Everyone stood in line
to get their lunch—barley soup and dry bread. The
musicians opened their suitcases. A smell of sawdust
and open roads swept through the long corridors.

Suddenly the old rabbi appeared in the street.
Many years ago they had brought him to Badenheim
from the east. For a few years he had officiated in the
local synagogue—or to tell the truth, the old-age
home. When the old men died the place was left
empty. The rabbi had a paralytic stroke. In the town
they were sure that he had died along with the other
old men.

The hotel owner stood in the doorway and said,
"Come in, sir," as if he were not the owner but the
doorman. Two musicians lifted the wheelchair. The
rabbi shaded his eyes and a blue vein throbbed on
his white forehead.

"Jews?" asked the rabbi.

"Jews," said the hotel owner.

"And who is your rabbi?" asked the rabbi.

"You, you are our rabbi."

The rabbi's face expressed a grim astonishment. His old memory tried to discover if they were making fun of him.

"Perhaps you will allow us to offer you something to drink?"

The rabbi frowned. "Kosher?" he asked.

The hotel owner dropped his eyes and did not reply.

"Are you all Jews here?" The old man recovered and a distant spark of cunning glinted in his eyes.

"All, I think."

"And what do you do?"

"Nothing," smiled the hotel owner.

Samitzky came to the rescue and said: "We're getting ready to return to Poland."

"What?" said the rabbi, straining to hear.

"To return to Poland," Samitzky repeated.

The next day the mystery cleared up a little. A Christian woman, a good woman, had looked after him all these years, but suddenly she had abandoned him. The rabbi spent a few days trying to move the wheelchair, and in the end he succeeded.

The rabbi asked questions and the people answered. The many years of isolation had made him forget the language, and he spoke a mixture of Yiddish and Hebrew. A number of musicians appeared in the doorway, suitcases in their hands.

"Who are they?" asked the rabbi.

"The musicians."

"Are they preparing to play?"

"No. They want to go home but the roads are blocked."

"Let them stay and spend the Sabbath with us, let them stay and spend the Sabbath."

"What did he say?" asked the musicians in surprise.

The leaden autumn light now ruled the town. The hotel owner stood in the kitchen like one of the servants dishing out the soup. No new supplies arrived. Stocks were running out. The dining room looked like a charity soup kitchen. And in the evening long shadows crept over the tables. A dumb awkwardness stared from the musicians' eyes. A few days ago they were still indignant. And now all their desires seemed to have been quenched. They understood: there was no more going back. Even Dr. Pappenheim's optimism faded. The pastry shop owner waved his fists in the direction of the hotel, in fact in the direction of Pappenheim, and vowed to kill him.

"What is the rabbi saying?" asked Frau Zauberblit.

"He's sleeping," whispered the hotel owner.

The musicians had no pity on the hotel owner and stuffed china dishes and silver cutlery into their bags. Samitzky reproached them: "What do you think you're doing? In Poland people don't eat from china plates."

"We're not doing anything wrong," said one of them, like a person caught stealing for the first time. "If we ever return, we'll give it all back."

The luxuriant creepers had crept inside and were now filling the verandah in a last burst of growth before the winter. The abandoned chairs stood dumbly in their places. The shade lay heavily on the geranium pots and the flowers were as red as rotten beets.

"What happened to the major?" asked someone.

"He shot himself."

Next to the closed shutters of the pastry shop stood Bertha Shtumglantz. She had been brought back to the town the day before. Her parents had died many years ago and the house had been transferred to the town council.

"Do you remember me?" asked Sally.

"I think so. Didn't we study together in the Gymnasium?"

"No, my dear, we didn't. My name is Sally and this is Gertie."

"I must be mistaken then," said Bertha apologetically.

"My name is Sally. This is Gertie."

Bertha did not remember. It was evident that her memory had abandoned her. Her eyes wandered about aimlessly.

"Why is everything closed?"

"The town is getting ready to be transferred. Dr. Pappenheim says that everyone is being transferred to Poland—us too."

"Dr. Pappenheim?"

"The impresario, don't you remember him?"

Strange people were brought in from the gates. Dr. Pappenheim stood at the hotel doorway like a doorman.

"Why had you come here?" asked someone.

"They were born here and they have to return here."

"It's not so bad here," intervened Pappenheim. "Mandelbaum is with us and so are the twins."

"The twins? Who are the twins?"

"Where are you from, Jews?" asked the rabbi as people used to ask in the old days. An ancient grief glazed his eyes.

"This is our rabbi," boasted Dr. Pappenheim. "A real rabbi of the old school."

The rabbi asked questions all the time. The hotel owner put on a skullcap and gave him cold water to drink.

Every day new people arrived, the descendants of old Badenheim families. The curse of the town had pursued them all these years and now it had finally caught up with them. They wandered about in the paralyzed void of the town like lost souls. In the middle of all this Dr. Pappenheim received a letter from the Sanitation Department demanding that he place all the artists registered with him at their disposal. Pappenheim was delighted: "A comprehensive concert tour awaits us!"

The autumn grew gray. The wind muttered in the empty streets. Mandelbaum tortured his trio mercilessly. He polished every note. The twins went into seclusion again. A grim atmosphere settled on the hotel. Pappenheim walked on tiptoe and whispered, "Shush, don't disturb the music." The musicians ate their bread silently. "Rehearsing won't help us anymore. What you failed to do when you were young you can't make up for later." Pappenheim was consoling: where they were going they would have lots of time, they would be able to practice. He too intended to get down to some serious research.

Dr. Pappenheim made constant attempts to communicate with the pastry shop owner. "Why are you angry with us? What have we done? We haven't done anything wrong. Tell us what we've done wrong. In Poland you'll be able to open a bigger pastry shop than this one. A man must broaden his horizons." But words were useless. The pastry shop owner stood next to the shuttered window and cursed. If it wasn't for the hotel, for the corruption, the authorities wouldn't have closed off the town. It was all because of Pappenheim. He ought to be arrested. Only at night did he fall silent.

Mandelbaum seemed better pleased. The trio filled him with enthusiasm. He himself was getting new sounds out of the violin.

"When are we leaving?" he asked Pappenheim, in the tone he sometimes used with his own agent.

"Soon," said Dr. Pappenheim, as if he had some secret information.

"We're improving you know, we're improving."

On Saturday night there was a heavy rainfall. The rabbi prayed aloud. The people hugged the walls like shadows. The hotel owner brought wine and candles and the rabbi made the blessing.

Straight after the blessing the musicians went upstairs to pack. Their suitcases were big and swollen. Dr. Pappenheim was surprised at all the commotion. "I'm going just as I am," he said, "without anything. If they want me they'll take me just as I am, without anything."

28

The last days of Badenheim were illuminated by a dull, yellow light. There were no more cigarettes. People fed in secret on the stolen drugs. Some were gay and others sunk into depression. The people stood by the windows or climbed to the upper floors. The recent rains had brought the autumn leaves in the Luxembourg Gardens to life. It was a splendid sight. And the hotel resembled a place of worship in which you could cry out or be silent and no one would ask you why.

The headwaiter was learning Yiddish. Samitzky wrote long lists of words down in his notebook and sat and studied them. He had started to walk with a stoop and stare into space. His Austrian accent clung to him like a leech but he tried his best to overcome this obstacle too. Salo consoled him, saying that in Poland it would be easy to learn. Everyone spoke Yiddish there.

"I find the language very interesting," said the headwaiter.

Martin was bowed down with grief. The pharmacy had been cleaned out by the looters. Cosmetics were strewn all over the floor, a testimony to the violence. All his pleas were in vain. The people avoided him as though he were a policeman.

The rabbi recovered. There was a look of cold sanity on his pale face. Pappenheim sat next to him and spoke eloquently: the people were going gladly to Poland. They were happy, looking forward to it eagerly.

"And what will you do there?"

"What do you mean?"

"Do the people intend to keep the commandments?" The rabbi smiled shrewdly, as if he knew that his question was indiscreet.

"The headwaiter is studying hard and I myself am now reading Buber's great work."

"Buber. At one time there was a lot of talk about him. So his books are still read?"

"I can promise you that the hostility toward the *Ostjuden* is a thing of the past." There was a pleading note in Dr. Pappenheim's voice, as if he were seeking the rabbi's blessing for the journey. But the rabbi was unbending.

"And how will you make a living?" he asked.

"There are great artists among us," said Dr. Pappenheim, his tongue coming back to life again, "artists of world stature. Dr. Shutz is a young mathematician of genius. Dr. Fussholdt is a famous historian."

Gaiety again gained the upper hand. Sally and Gertie put on their best clothes. Salo made jokes all the time. Even the wretched Mitzi laughed to split her sides. Martin's pills succeeded where the artists had failed. Only Martin's sorrow knew no bounds. He recited all the drugs of death by their Latin and German names. But his was a voice calling in the wilderness.

On Karl the drugs apparently had a bad effect. He was angry. His eyes flickered with a strange flame. Lotte did not stir from his side, but he could not control himself and all his anger was directed against Dr. Langmann. "Sport he wants to introduce. Sport!"

"What does the rabbi say?" the people asked.

"A wonderful man," said Pappenheim proudly.

The musicians were miserable now. They had robbed the hotel, packed their bags, accumulated fortunes; now they lay in bed at night munching chocolate. But these secret feasts did not bring them any joy. They seemed like thieves in their own eyes and they were afraid, simply afraid. Samitzky remembered a song people had sung in Poland when he was a child, and the tune took hold of him like fire. It spread with a kind of fierce intensity. Gertie rolled on the floor like a ball and nobody seemed surprised.

The drugs ran out and the people sank into themselves, into their sadness. Despair now stared from every wall. The kitchen was dark, the tea tables were deserted, and the two chandeliers hung askew, like the morning after a wild party. What could be done? What could be remedied? If only the Festival could be revived! Was there no chance of reviving the Festival? Mandelbaum tyrannized his musicians and refused to leave his room. The twins said that they would appear in Warsaw when they reached Poland. The yanuka was behaving like a

133

spoiled child. He would only sing for boxes of candy. His cheeks grew pale. He grew fat. He had apparently lost his voice. Without music and with no means of breathing life into the people, the performers withdrew into themselves.

Dr. Pappenheim stood at the hotel gates and held forth to the strangers. Someone asked for information about the Festival. Pappenheim apologized for the confusion in the schedule. He had done everything in his power, but what could he do if this year other matters had taken precedence?

If only the Festival could be revived! Was there no way in which the Festival could be revived? The people now dogged Dr. Pappenheim's footsteps not with demands but with pleas. The drug they had become accustomed to over the years, it was this drug they now craved above all. Dr. Pappenheim stood by the great artist's door and begged: "Just one concert, just one, have mercy on us. . . ."

29

There was no end to surprises: Helena returned. She stood at the gate in a long dress with a shawl over her head, like a peasant woman turned out by her husband. She entered the town and the sentries did not ask her where she was going. She walked slowly down the street like someone returning without joy or desire to an old home. For a moment she stood outside the looted pharmacy, and then she went inside.

"Helena," said Trude without any particular surprise, as if Helena had just come home from school.

Helena drew up a chair and sat down.

The night before Trude had sat in the armchair murmuring to herself: "When will Helena return? Tomorrow or the day after. She is already on her way to us." Martin no longer questioned her. Her disease had filled him completely. She spoke about

the town of her birth in Poland as if she had left it
only a few weeks before, and once she had even
approached Samitzky and spoken to him in Polish.
Samitzky was overjoyed to hear his native tongue
and he struck up an animated conversation with
her. Frau Zauberblit stood to one side and mar-
veled at the fondness they felt for their native
tongue.

Helena sat without speaking. Trude asked neither
how nor why. Martin went down on his knees and
kissed her hands and in his embarrassment he said,
"Mother keeps on saying, Helena's on her way,
Helena's on her way. . . ."

"Father is excited," said Trude. "See how excited
he is."

Now Martin knew that everything Trude said was
true. And the sorrow he had borne within him for
many days melted into tears.

"What was it like?" asked Martin, as if he were
asking about some excursion or exam. "We were a
little worried."

"I was not worried," said Trude.

"Your mother is very glad to be returning to the
town of her birth in Poland."

And in the evening Martin gave them tea and
cookies. It was like old times. Helena took the
peasant shawl off her head and her high forehead transmitted a kind of dry sorrow. She stirred
her tea and the sounds died down one after another.

"We're leaving," said Trude. "Your father has
already wound up his affairs."

Helena raised her eyes and gave them a long,
caressing look.

"A goy will always be a goy. And your goy too is a goy. I'm not sorry," said Trude.

Helena dropped her eyes.

"I am right, yes?" said Trude. The subject was an old one that had never been discussed openly in the house.

30

The dogs tried to jump over the walls but they did not have the strength. The sentries drove them back in. They grew very gaunt and hostile to people. The headwaiter patted them gently and said that if they behaved themselves and were obedient he would take them to Poland. It all depended on them. The dogs could not understand what was happening. The angry glare in their eyes shone like polished metal.

And at night they tore the silence to shreds. The people had nightmares. Mitzi said that she had never had such terrible nightmares in all her life. Salo interpreted her dreams favorably and said that it was all because of the dogs—if it weren't for the dogs they could all sleep in peace, the mild autumn air was good for sleep.

Dr. Langmann was no longer indignant. He sat in an armchair and looked at the people, putting a word in every now and then. The people did not bother him. Even Karl no longer seemed to feel hostility toward him. But Mandelbaum was very angry with the dogs. He kept emerging from his room and thundering, "Quiet, barbarians! They should be destroyed." The pastry shop owner had shut himself up. The old pastry cook stood in the doorway in his pressed suit and stared into space. The long years by the ovens had left him with no will of his own. Salo explained to him that it was necessary to improve economic and social conditions. The worker was exploited. In Poland there was a militant proletariat which fought for its place in industry. It needed courage of course, but once you overcame your initial fear you could see how stupid you had been in the past. When the pastry shop owner overheard he told the old pastry cook not to pay any attention to clowns. All that was needed was to send the *Ostjuden* back to the east. In recent years they had been flooding Austria.

"What about the hotel owner?" asked the old man.

"The hotel owner is an Austrian, that's true, but he was weak and opened the door to that buffoon, Dr. Pappenheim, the arch *Ostjude* and source of all our troubles. Who invented the Festival if not Pappenheim? Who filled the town with morbid artists and decadent vacationers?"

"And what about me?" asked the pastry cook.

"You were born here; your parents were born here. You are of the Jewish faith but not an *Ostjude*."

The pastry cook was happy. The pastry shop owner had never taken the trouble to talk to him before. All these years he had treated him harshly and in the summer season he had worked him like a slave. But now he sat and talked to him like a human being.

"And who brought Sally and Gertie here?" inquired the pastry cook.

"What do you mean who brought them? Pappenheim of course! Don't you remember, he tried to pass them off as singers. I at any rate never allowed them to cross the threshold of my shop."

The headwaiter could no longer control the dogs. Their hostility toward the people grew more bitter by the day. They fell on Lotte and tore her dress. Karl swore to himself that he would poison them.

The headwaiter implored them: "After all, you aren't wild animals. If you keep on behaving like this I won't be able to take you to Poland. All these years I've been feeding you and now, when I have no food to give you, you don't want to listen to me anymore."

"What can I do?" the headwaiter said in despair to the people.

"The pastry shop owner will look after them. He's staying, isn't he?"

"He hates them."

The autumn flowers were already filling the air with their pungent scents and the leaden sun shone steadily above the high windows, climbing slowly and sucking the shade up into itself. The tennis court was covered with yellow leaves and looked like an abandoned field.

"What can I do? I can't control them anymore," muttered the headwaiter to himself. "If only I had some fresh meat perhaps I'd be able to influence them—they're only dogs, after all."

And when the sun sank and the light of the night

fell on the street the pastry shop owner stuck his head out of the window and shouted loudly: "It's all Dr. Pappenheim's fault. I would never have let him in in the first place. Let him go east—the east is the right place for him. We haven't done anyone any harm." There was a stubborn rhythm in his voice and from the hotel lobby it sounded like someone shouting slogans over a loudspeaker. In the end he withdrew his head and a heavy silence descended with the darkness and enfolded the people huddled in the corners of the lobby.

31

And there was no end to surprises. One night two guards from the sanitorium appeared to take Frau Zauberblit back to the institution. They had searched for a long time and now that they had found her they were happy. Frau Zauberblit was not surprised: like an escaped convict she was prepared for anything, and for this bitter possibility too.

The two aged guards looked healthy and robust in their sanitorium uniforms. One was carrying a leather briefcase which held a search warrant and an order for administrative arrest.

"How did you find me in this Godforsaken hole?" she laughed.

"We searched for a long time," they said without anger.

In recent days her cough had grown worse, there was more blood in her phlegm, and the pains in her

back were very bad. Her medicines were running
out, and Death came back to her in exactly the same
guise he had worn in the sanitorium.

"Why don't you sit down? It's such a long time
since we've seen each other," said Frau Zauberblit,
as if she were talking to old friends.

"Our sanitorium is emigrating too."

"The Jewish patients."

When she was first hospitalized the guards were
still young men. The female patients used to flirt
with them. They liked the peasant in them. The
years passed and they too grew old, but their robust
health did not leave them. Their faces were ruddy
with sausages and beer.

"I'm already registered here, you know, with the
esteemed Sanitation Department."

"Why not come with everyone else?" they said in
kind, fatherly tones.

Dr. Pappenheim rushed to her aid, but the aged
guards, who looked like two men of God on a
religious mission, explained calmly that all the Jewish patients had already been assembled and only
Frau Zauberblit was missing. The transport could
not leave without her.

"Only I am missing?" she exclaimed. "In that
case, let's go. They say that the air in Poland is
purer. I need pure air."

"That's what our doctors say, too."

"If so, let's go," said Frau Zauberblit. "Let's go
back to the sanitorium. People have to go back to
where they came from. So they say, if I'm not
mistaken."

"Have you no suitcase?" asked the guards. "It's
chilly in the evening."

"What's the hurry?" Dr. Pappenheim tried to

delay the departure. "We're all going to the same place."

"The sanitorium patients are traveling under medical supervision," said one of them gently.

"You're leaving us then?" There was an imploring note in Dr. Pappenheim's voice.

"Not for long."

Frau Zauberblit put on her summer dress and said, "I'm ready."

"Isn't that dress too thin?" one of them asked again in the voice of a concerned old friend.

"I can't endure heavy clothes. Did a lot of people run away this year?"

"Only five. We've brought them all back. They have to go to Poland too."

Samitzky was asleep in the Luxembourg Gardens. All night long he had been drinking and quarreling with the pastry cook, cursing Karl and threatening to break the aquarium. In the morning he fell exhausted onto a bench in the park. All attempts to wake him were in vain. He slept deeply.

"Let's go then," she said. "Why should we stand here doing nothing?" A sick beauty bloomed in her face. The people accompanied her to the gate. She kissed the yanuka on the forehead and said, "I expect great things of you." No carriage stood waiting. They walked off in the direction of the station. The autumn light, the leaden light, dominated the fields. The effects of the rain were already apparent in the town pasture. Here and there a horse or cow grazed. And the river was like a ribbon of silver. "Isn't it beautiful?" Frau Zauberblit asked the guards.

When Samitzky woke and they told him, he said nothing. In the evening he smashed the glass of the back door. The splinters were scattered everywhere. The hotel owner did not hurry to the scene. The people knew that the man's pain was greater than he was, and that there was no consolation.

The old pastry cook had freed himself of the yoke of the pastry shop owner. At night he buried the dead in the back of the Luxembourg Gardens. There was a kind of calm detachment in his movements, as if he had been a gravedigger all his life. Every day more people were crowded in. The new people were so feeble and withdrawn, they were like birds who had lost contact with the sky. They died silently, without crying out. The old pastry cook prepared them for burial and buried them at night.

32

On the last night they celebrated Gertie's fortieth birthday. Sally and Gertie decorated their house in honor of their guests. It was an old-fashioned country cottage, well preserved and adorned with rose bushes. Inside a feminine softness reigned. Here counts, Grafs, industrialists, and various tired intellectuals had found a lodging for the night. True, the house was no longer what it had been. They did their best to give the parlor the air of feminine softness they liked. But to no avail. The house now looked like a shabby roadside inn. A gray light poured from the lamps and spilled onto the floor. The heavy carpet looked very worn.

Dr. Pappenheim came first. He kissed Gertie's cheeks and said in a festive tone, "It's been a long time since I was last here."

They were as pleased as if it were not the familiar Dr. Pappenheim but a visitor from far away. "I am

147

the bearer of important news today;" he added. "The emigration procedures have already been posted on the notice boards."

"What do you say!" said Gertie.

Dr. Shutz and the schoolgirl arrived next. The schoolgirl wore a long blue dress in honor of the occasion. She was taller than Shutz by a head. There was a quiet authority in her bearing. Shutz drew up a chair for her and she sat down. Sally and Gertie withdrew a little, as from a stranger.

On the low table they had spread an embroidered cloth. In the corner was a vase with dried flowers. A delicate scent of feminine perfumes pervaded the air.

"Have you heard?" said Gertie. "The emigration procedures have been posted on the notice boards."

Dr. Langmann came in stooping from the back entrance. Karl's stares pursued him all the time. Perhaps here he would be free of them. He had found a big bottle of liqueur and brought it to the party. He kissed Gertie's hand and said, "How nice it is here. Karl refuses to budge from the aquarium. What does he want of the fish? What harm have they done anyone?"

"He changes the water and feeds them bread crumbs," said the schoolgirl in a cool, grave voice.

Dr. Langmann looked at her suspiciously.

Dr. Pappenheim had done his best to persuade Mandelbaum to come to the party, but his pleas had fallen on deaf ears. The great artist was making his last effort, he explained. But the twins had agreed to come. They had dressed the yanuka in a new suit, and he sat in an armchair like an adult.

Gertie was very embarrassed and kept on saying, "Excuse me." Sally, who was two years older, for some reason now seemed like Gertie's aunt. Sally's legs had swollen and were ravaged by varicose veins.

Salo came too. He said that Karl was preparing to take the fish with him. He kept poking about in the aquarium. Nobody laughed. Gertie's embarrassment continued to embarrass her guests until Dr. Pappenheim rose and said that the time had come to drink a toast in honor of the occasion.

Salo approached Dr. Langmann and whispered, "There's no help for it, everyone has to go."

Dr. Langmann did not reply.

"There's nothing to be afraid of. In Poland there are lots of Jews. The Jews help each other, you know."

Dr. Langmann again ignored his whispers, but Salo would not leave him alone. "I come from there," he went on in the same whisper. "I spent my childhood and youth in Poland. I know them well. A year or two among them and you'll forget everything. You'll get up in the morning and go to synagogue. Is that bad? You'll pray. Is that bad? Is it a sin to pray? And if you're lucky enough to have a shop in the center of town you'll earn a good living too. Even the peddlers make a living. My father was a peddler and my mother had a stall in the marketplace. We were a lot of kids at home. Too many. I was the seventh. Are you listening to me?"

"No," said Dr. Langmann with loathing.

"Don't put on airs. You're going to my birthplace and motherland. All I'm trying to do is give you a little information. I'd advise you to leave your arrogant ways behind you. In Poland people treat each other with respect."

Sally approached the twins and said, "How can we gladden the hearts of the artists?" The twins now looked like monks. Their hair grew wildly on their heads. They sat in a corner and did not open their mouths. Mitzi laughed. Every word that was said aroused her laughter. "Why are you laughing?" asked Sally.

"For no reason. Just because people make me laugh."

But the liqueur did not bring gaiety. The people sank deeper into the armchairs. The light from the lamps poured onto the floor as from a broken tube. The colored wall, adorned with reproductions, seemed to come alive: it was as if dormant veins had started to throb in it. Nocturnal shadows slunk against the windows and a fat fly beat against the screen. If there were any words left they belonged to Salo. But Salo did not speak. A kind of smile split open on his forehead. An evil smile, smeared there with poisonous paint.

The lights grew dimmer, and delicate sounds invaded the room from outside. It seemed that the country parlor was already living a life of its own, a life without people.

"The emigration procedures seem very efficient— very efficient indeed, if I may say so," said Dr. Pappenheim.

"In that case, our expectations were not in vain," said Dr. Shutz.

"Very efficient indeed," repeated Pappenheim.

"You'll be able to teach in the mathematics department," said Salo to Dr. Shutz. "Poland is a cultured country."

"Are they connected to the University of Vienna?" inquired Dr. Shutz.

"I imagine so," said Salo. "All centers of culture are connected to Vienna or Berlin."

They had another drink. The liqueur was sweet and had a cloying, disagreeable taste. Old words came floating to the surface, and old faces. "The Bluebird," for example, and the deceiver who had stood in the courtyard proclaiming at the top of his voice, "Save your souls before it's too late!"

"Tell me, Dr. Pappenheim, how did it all end, that strange affair?" asked Gertie, with an affectation of interest, in the same manner in which she had probably once asked counts about their business affairs.

"What do you mean?" said Dr. Pappenheim. "I asked Professor Fussholdt to testify on my behalf. He made a brilliant speech."

"How interesting," said Gertie in the same affected tone. "And you were acquitted, of course."

"I, to tell the truth, suspected him all along," said Sally.

"An engaging rogue, a prophet and lecher at one and the same time!" said Dr. Pappenheim.

The headwaiter sat in a corner, elegant in his black suit. He wore this black suit rarely, keeping it for special occasions. For some reason he looked like a man in whom the fire of life has died down. He looked ill at ease, and from time to time he wiped his high red forehead with a folded handkerchief. He listened to the conversation without taking part in it, as if they were speaking of matters too weighty for him.

Gertie stood in the kitchen doorway and apologized. "I feel so ashamed. We have nothing to offer you."

"Never mind," said Pappenheim. "We'll take a raincheck for a party in Warsaw, a lavish party."

"I promise," said Gertie.

Pappenheim sipped the liqueur and returned to his theme. "In Poland we'll be able to diversify our Festival. There's a wealth of folklore there, authentic folklore."

"Of course," interrupted Salo, "I myself once saw a wonderful play in Yiddish, *Bontze the Silent* I think it was called. My father took me."

"What do you say, Dr. Langmann? East and West will be as one!" said Dr. Pappenheim.

Dr. Langmann removed his empty pipe from his mouth and spat out, "Cheap romanticism!"

They sat and chatted. Their voices mingled. The main speaker was Salo and all he wanted was to annoy Dr. Langmann, but Dr. Langmann seemed indifferent to his taunts.

It was late. Dr. Pappenheim rose and said: "Good-by, house; au revoir, house. You're staying here and we're setting off on our travels. Au revoir, maidens, until tomorrow morning at seven o'clock sharp on the hotel steps."

The damp night air struck them in the face. In Mandelbaum's window the lights were off. The music was stilled. Karl stood poring over the aquarium as if he were registering every delicate vibration in the green water. Lotte sat in the armchair and watched him. The people walked slowly down the street. There was dew on the paving stones and the air was dense with the mossy smell of the autumn forests. No one mentioned the name of Frau Milbaum. For two weeks now she had not been seen in the lobby. The thought that she was sitting enthroned in her room—a body without a soul—this thought was too terrible to put into words.

The looted pharmacy looked like a dark, gaping cave. The ripped-out shutter lying in the gutter turned its ragged edge, all bent out of shape, toward the street with the grim expression peculiar to metal. Trude sat in an armchair and leafed through a magazine. Helena's homecoming had revived in her the familiar movements of the past. Her happiness was drugged and expressionless.

"The musicians, my musicians, have looted the hotel," recalled Dr. Pappenheim and burst out laughing.

The pastry shop was overgrown with creepers. The streetlight illuminated the bushes and the fallen leaves. The house itself was sunk in total darkness.

"What do you say to a strawberry tart and a cup of coffee?" said Mitzi.

"I'd give the world for them," said Salo.

They walked on toward the Luxembourg Gardens. The dogs stood next to the streetlight. They stood without moving. There was a kind of yearning in their silent gaze. They had grown thinner than the people. The headwaiter crushed stale bread in water for them, but they could not digest it. They had tried to break out of the town several times, but the sentries had stopped them. Two had been shot, and the two survivors seemed to understand that their own fate would be no different from that of their fellows. You could see that they wanted to die, but Death did not seem to want them yet. Ever since the death of their friends they had stopped begging and fawning; they had retreated into the bushes and waited for Death, and because Death did not come for them they came out and stood under the light.

The headwaiter approached the bushes. For a moment his eyes met theirs and he cried: "Who wants to come with me to Poland?" The dogs did not stir.

"I'm giving you one more chance," said the headwaiter in a thin but very clear voice. "Who wants to come with me to Poland?"

"I see that you prefer to stay here then," he said and turned his back on them.

"Ingrates," whispered Pappenheim. "They're only dogs, after all."

"I'm not angry with them," said the headwaiter. "They're in mourning."

There was a wind blowing in the Luxembourg Gardens and delicate shadows, forest shadows, netted the ancient cobblestones. Behind the park, in the nebulous darkness, a number of figures crowded together. They looked as insubstantial as the shadows dancing by their sides. "We must get some sleep," said Dr. Pappenheim. "It's a long trip to Poland." They went in through the back door so as not to encounter Karl's glare. Karl was sitting in an armchair with Lotte, not far from the aquarium.

Sally and Gertie stood watching their guests walk away. They were afraid of being alone in their house. In the bedrooms everything was upside down.

"I think we should just leave everything as it is. What have we got anyway? A lot of old party dresses and nighties," said Gertie, who was exhausted.

"We'd better take a look first." Sally attempted a practical tone.

"I've got no more feeling left for this house at all. Did you notice that the schoolgirl didn't utter a word all night? She hates us."

"Pregnant women are always spiteful."

"Poor Shutz looks so crushed next to her. You can't imagine how crushed he is. And he used to be such a high-spirited boy."

"Yes, I noticed. She rules him with a rod of iron."

The cases were not packed. The room filled up again with the heavy female perfumes. Gertie sank onto the sofa and fell asleep and Sally covered her with a woolen blanket. Sally was afraid to sleep alone in the untidy bedroom. She opened the folding bed and pulled it up to the sofa. Gertie's sleep was profound and completely detached from the outside world. "Everything's over," said Sally to herself, and passed her hand over Gertie's cool forehead.

33

The next day was clear and cold. Mandelbaum rose early and stood with his trio on the smooth hotel steps. His white suit gave him a casual, sporty air, but the weeks he had spent shut up in his room had left their mark. His face looked drained. There was a darting, nervous look in his eyes, as if he were suffering from an attack of the jitters before an important performance. The trio, also dressed in white suits, stood silently by his side. In the course of the years they had spent with Mandelbaum they had lost their freedom of movement. They stood and looked at the view. The morning was fine and feathery plumes of light covered the roof tiles. The air was cool and fresh.

"Where's the carriage?" Mandelbaum cried suddenly.

Dr. Pappenheim, who was used to responding to the artists' every caprice, came out immediately and said, "The emigration arrangements are evidently not yet complete."

"In that case we'll have to waste our time here doing nothing," said Mandelbaum. There was no anger in his voice. He seemed quite content. The trio had accomplished the possible and even the impossible. "And the pastry shop, what's happened to the pastry shop?"

"Everything has been closed down in readiness for the emigration," explained Dr. Pappenheim.

"In that case, we'll have to wait for coffee until we get to Warsaw," said Mandelbaum and turned back to his trio.

"Has the maestro already appeared in Warsaw?" inquired Dr. Pappenheim.

"A couple of times. An enthusiastic and sensitive audience, more so than the Austrians, I should say."

"I'm glad to hear it," said Dr. Pappenheim.

While they were talking Dr. Shutz and the schoolgirl appeared. The schoolgirl was wearing the same long dress she had worn the night before. Her whole bearing bespoke pride, the pride of a woman who has taken her fate into her own hands and has no regrets. Shutz looked weak and feeble next to her. The last bloom of youth had vanished from his face. A network of wrinkles lined his temples. He was still slender, but he had started walking with a slight stoop. He wore a heavy winter coat.

"Allow me to introduce Dr. Shutz," said Dr. Pappenheim.

"Honored," said Mandelbaum; and Shutz, who was carrying a wicker basket on his arm, fumbled awkwardly over the handshake.

"This is my wife," he said in embarrassment.

The schoolgirl turned away with an angry, reproving expression on her face.

For a moment it seemed that the light carriages, the splendid opera carriages, were about to appear. What a festive hour that always was! The feathery frost glittered on the roofs in a last burst of radiance. The low houses seemed a little bowed, as if someone had draped them in an old fishing net. There was nobody standing at the gates and in Sally and Gertie's house a window hung open.

All night long Karl had struggled to uproot the aquarium, but the accursed screws had rusted. In the end, after the old saw too had failed him, he took the fish out and put them in a bottle. It wasn't an easy job. Lotte helped him. Now he too stood on the smooth steps holding the bottle wrapped in a green sweater. He cradled it in his arms like a sleeping baby. Lotte stationed herself by his side, ready to humor him. "Perhaps you should bring an extra bottle of water," he said to her. It was evident that she had now surrendered completely to his madness. She went back inside and Karl removed the sweater and scrutinized the fish.

"Dr. Pappenheim, so we're late as usual," said Mandelbaum. The word *late* was always on his lips. Sometimes it was he himself who was late and sometimes it was the carriage that was late in coming for him. Even though Mandelbaum knew that this time their departure was not dependent on the impresario the words escaped him as if by force of habit.

Mitzi was wearing a green flowered dress. She had spent the whole night making her face up. The disappointments of the season had been somewhat erased from her face, and a new expectation had taken their place. Her husband, Professor Fussholdt, was still busy packing the proofs of his book. Dr. Pappenheim introduced her to Mandelbaum. Mandelbaum said in great surprise, "Professor Fussholdt! So Professor Fussholdt is with us too!"

"Professor Fussholdt has been busy this season proofreading his latest book," said Dr. Pappenheim, "a massive work."

"What a shame that I didn't know," said Mandelbaum regretfully.

Mitzi was silent. The mention of her husband's name by Mandelbaum, and with such reverence, was not particularly pleasing to her. Then she said, "He'll be down in a little while. He's busy packing his proofs."

The hotel owner stood in the doorway. All that was left of his impressive appearance was his silver hair, and that was very striking now. There was a quiet sadness in his green eyes. The musicians emerged from the lower floor. They were dragging their heavy bags, their loot. Dr. Pappenheim had spoken to them at length, but their greed was stronger than they were. The conductor had broken off relations with them. But the hotel owner himself was not angry with them. He stood at the door and his sad eyes were full of resignation.

The headwaiter came out with a dog. That night the third dog had died, and in the morning the solitary survivor had responded at last to his blandishments. The musicians, who had accumulated large stocks of food, gave him a tin of sardines. The starving dog did not want to eat, he only drank. And the headwaiter packed a suitcase. At first he had thought of setting out without any luggage, but the sudden coming of the dog had made him change his mind. He decided to pack a medium-sized suitcase. He also managed to wash and comb the dog, who now looked thin but neat.

"I see the dog agreed to come in the end," said Mitzi.

"He was left all alone."

"But there were two dogs last night, weren't there?"

"Yes, but one of them was shot."

"You don't say so! What's this one's name?"

"Lutzi."

"I could never tell them apart. Lutzi, you say?"

"Each of them had his own personality. They were all different. Lutzi was always the quietest of them all. A dog with a lot of complexes, if I may be permitted to use the expression. Am I right, Lutzi?"

The dog did not react.

"And so Lutzi decided to come to Poland. Strange. He must have decided this morning then?"

"For my part," said the headwaiter, "I would have been quite prepared to take them all, but they apparently couldn't face the move."

"What a pity," said Mitzi insincerely.

Salo too had not slept all night. He was wearing his old suit, his traveling-salesman's suit with the faded label of his firm. On his cap there was a "W" made of metal. Once he had looked very young in this uniform, but now he looked stooped and worn out. "When are we leaving?" he asked, but no one answered him. He put his suitcase down on one side. It was a rather battered old case which had recently been stamped with the letter "W" and a serial number. Salo rushed frantically to and fro like a mole exposed to the light of day. In the end he went and stood at the entrance to the bottom floor, next to the musicians. The musicians were sitting on the floor leaning against their bulging luggage.

Sally and Gertie dressed the yanuka. The hotel owner had found a child's suit of winter clothing for him in the stores. The suit fitted him. They even found a hat, a hat with a feather. "Why, you're a prince, a fairy prince!" said Gertie. The time he had spent in Badenheim had changed him. The flickering fear had disappeared from his eyes. He had grown fat, his cheeks had grown pink, and he had learned to understand German. His voice had apparently been lost altogether, and the few things he remembered about his home, his parents, and the orphanage in Vienna were quite gone. He was already speaking with an Austrian accent and behaving like a spoiled child. Sally found shoe polish and polished his shoes. The yanuka did not say thank you or laugh. He was too busy devouring chocolates. Ever since he had discovered the taste of candy, he had not stopped gorging. The people brought him presents to placate him and he had become used to accepting these presents as his due. Any innocence he might once have had was quite gone now. He understood that Sally and Gertie had never studied at the university, and that the schoolgirl was carrying Dr. Shutz's child and was really not his wife. Salo appeared and the yanuka cried, "Salo, what do you think of my clothes? Sally and Gertie say that I look like a fairy prince."

"They're quite right."

"In that case," said the yanuka, "the prince commands you to give him the box of candy he sees sticking out of your pocket."

"That's not a box of candy, my dear," said Salo in

surprise. "It's only a pair of stockings, women's stockings—I'm the agent for a well-known firm."

At that moment the rabbi's voice was heard.

"Are you leaving me here?"

Dr. Pappenheim, who was absorbed in his conversation with Mandelbaum, nevertheless hurried to the door and said, "We're all here still, we're all here. It's cold outside."

"Please be good enough to take me out of here," said the rabbi, taking no notice at all of Dr. Pappenheim's excuses. There was a secret suspicion in the old man's heart. He seemed alert, with the alertness of a sick man already past feeling pain. Dr. Pappenheim took hold of the handles of the wheelchair and pushed him to the doorway.

The sun came down from the trees and spread itself over the paving stones of the Luxembourg Gardens. The fountains, which had not been working for a long time, suddenly began spurting jets of water. The sunlit water rose high in the air and fell with a heavy noise. Perhaps the taps of the pool had been opened too, for the schoolgirl turned her head—or more precisely her nose—to the right, in the direction of the pool, as if she smelled water.

The headwaiter stroked Lutzi and tried to feed him dry biscuits, but the dog refused to eat. Karl approached the headwaiter, removed the sweater from the bottle, and asked him for his advice. The headwaiter expressed the opinion that if the journey was not too long it might be possible to save the fish. "I've got an extra bottle of water," said Karl. And while they were all busy talking, the hotel owner descended the steps and walked over to the pastry shop. He stopped by the drawn shutter and called, "Peter, aren't you coming with us?"

Everyone froze in their places. Nobody had expected a gesture of this nature from the hotel owner. There was no reply from inside the house. The hotel owner repeated, more loudly than before, "Peter, you're contravening a municipal ordinance. You're taking a heavy responsibility on yourself."

After a moment of silence the voice of the pastry shop owner was heard. "I'm not coming. Not with Pappenheim anyway."

"You're an intelligent man," the hotel owner called again, as calmly as he could. "How can you take such a heavy responsibility on yourself?"

"I'm staying here."

"If you'll take my advice," said the hotel owner very gently, "I'd advise you to join us. You know very well that I only want your own good. We have a rabbi with us. He's coming too. If he has agreed to join us, why don't you come too?"

"I'm not religious," stated the voice from within.

There was a silence. The hotel owner started back toward the steps.

"Why is he always picking on me? What have I ever done to him? I've never harmed him," mumbled Dr. Pappenheim.

"He's angry," said Mandelbaum. It was obvious that he was thinking about something else. His body was full of music again. His feet tapped lightly on the steps, as if of their own accord. The trio also tapped silently with their feet. The same tune had evidently begun to play in their heads too.

"What does he want of me?" Dr. Pappenheim repeated, but his voice was so quiet that nobody heard him.

It was eight o'clock already but there did not seem to be any movement at the gates. The empty houses exuded silence and morning vapors rose from the patches of light. There were many shadows, and they crowded round the corners of the houses, cowering together. The water from the fountains rose high into the air. Nobody ever saw the morning hours in Badenheim, especially at this season of the year. They were all asleep.

"Aren't you taking any luggage?" Salo asked Dr. Pappenheim.

It was already eight o'clock and nothing was happening. It reminded Salo of the army. You lay in the dugouts for hours at a time. The regimental officers went to parties in town and the junior officers sat in the staff headquarters drinking beer. The NCOs were only too happy to have nothing to do, and the troops lay in the dugouts.

"Is that what it was like in the First World War?"

"Yes, exactly. And it seems to me that that's what it's going to be like now too. We'll have to get used to the new way of life."

34

At last the signal was given. Mandelbaum ran lightly down the steps, like an athlete, and stood at the head. Strangely enough, there were no traces of his weeks of strict seclusion left now. The trio stationed themselves next to him, haggard and obedient. After them came the twins, and Sally and Gertie with the yanuka between them. Dr. Langmann stood in a row by himself. The heavy musicians, burdened with their clumsy bundles, hung back, afraid of being in the front rows. The conductor ignored them. He was now completely absorbed in conversation with the half-Jewish waitress. The waitress walked leaning on a wooden cane, holding herself erect.

"It's a pretty view, isn't it?" said the conductor. He had always been a man of few words, and now the ones he wanted seemed to be evading him out of spite.

The wet green fields lay spread around them. A delicate morning mist rose languidly in the air. How easy the transition was—they hardly felt it. The hotel owner pushed the rabbi's wheelchair as if he had been born to the task. No one offered to help him.

In the dull confusion of the last days a strange relationship had grown up between the waitress and the conductor. When she was ill the conductor had been to visit her and they had exchanged a few words. Ever since then they had not stopped thinking of each other. The night before, when everyone was celebrating at Sally and Gertie's, they sat together in the Luxembourg Gardens. He was as shy as a child and she laughed. He told her about his inheritance and savings, all the confidential details that had accumulated in his systematic mind.

"So you're a rich man," she said.

After years of living inside himself, nagging his musicians and balancing his petty accounts, he now felt for the first time that the chains had fallen from his hands. She spoke of the journey, the new way of life. Of her Austrian father she spoke with a kind of contempt, as if he were not a man but a beast.

Now they walked together. The fields rolled away into the distance. There was no sound but the whispering footsteps. The policemen walked a little distance behind, without urging them on. Professor Fussholdt was happy. He had finished proofreading his new book. The pages were tied in a bundle with thick string. Mandelbaum walked by his side and asked him questions. Professor Fussholdt imitated the rhetoric of the Jewish functionaries who imagined that they were bringing the Messiah with their speeches. His hostility to everything considered Jewish culture, Jewish art, was lighter now. The bitterness and mockery had been buried in his book. Mitzi walked behind him like a stranger. The longer they walked the more his eloquence flowed, full of ingenious puns, witticisms, and plays on words. For months he had not spoken to a soul and now the words poured out of him.

The rabbi dozed in his wheelchair. The column of people approached the country cottages. The smell of morning milk and manure mingled in the air. Next to the oak tree the nature lovers had once paused to listen to the bird calls. Here "the Bluebird" once stood and made his inspiring speeches.

Salo did not seem at home on the open road he was so used to. For years he had traversed these fields with his medium-sized suitcase. The farmers, to tell the truth, did not like him. They always bought on credit and never paid their debts. His nonchalance suddenly deserted him. He huddled up to the musicians. The musicians sheltered him.

"The conductor hates us. What harm have we ever done him?" said the musician Zimbelman.

"Don't pay him any attention," said Salo.

"Even the hotel owner doesn't hate us."

"He'll come round. He won't have any alternative. You're his musicians after all, and he hasn't got any others besides you. By the way, did you get Pappenheim to sign Form 101?"

"No," said Zimbelman, "we forgot."

"That's a pity. Form 101's a good form, it gives you a lot of benefits."

"Dr. Pappenheim's always been very good to us. He even promoted us. We didn't dare ask."

"That's very important," said Salo. "In the end,

salary scales are the same everywhere. He promoted you to Musicians, eleventh grade, didn't he? A very decent grade."

"For myself," said Zimbelman, "I would like to work fewer hours. The drums drive me out of my mind. I'd be glad to take a year or two's leave. Believe me, I need it."

"I believe you. But the years on the threshold of retirement are critical. It's better to keep your rights. For my part I'd also take an early pension if it was up to me, but my firm's very strict, they suck the workers dry. I've already collected twenty years of seniority without missing a day. I've got a month's annual leave coming to me. I promised my wife a holiday in Majorca. Believe me, I deserve it."

"Majorca?" said Zimbelman. "I've never heard of it."

"A warm, wonderful island. I owe it to her. She brought the children up. Wonderful children."

"Do you think we'll be able to save something in Poland?" asked Zimbelman.

"Of course. Prices there are much lower, and if we go on getting our salaries in Austrian currency, we'll be able to save a lot."

The fields grew greener and greener. The pasture was cut into squares; they looked as if they had been measured with a ruler. A horse grazed in the field and a farmer's wife stood at her door. That was the way it had always been and that was the way it was now too.

"How strange it is," said the waitress, and tears came into her eyes.

"What do you mean?" said the conductor. "This is only a transition. Soon we'll arrive in Poland. New sights, new people. A man must broaden his horizons, no?"

"And I feel so bad, so like nothing at all."

"It's only a transition, only a transition. Soon we'll reach the station, the kiosk. I'm very partial to the lemonade, it's a local brand, very tasty." The words that had been buried in him for years suddenly blossomed. He wanted to lavish words on her. But the ones that he had in his possession did not seem able, for some reason, to combine into coherent sentences.

The rabbi woke from his slumbers and said aloud: "What do they want? All these years they haven't paid any attention to the Torah. Me they locked away in an old-age home. They didn't want to have anything to do with me. Now they want to go to Poland. There is no atonement without asking forgiveness first."

The rabbi's voice took the column of people by surprise. He spoke in a jumble of Hebrew and Yiddish. The people could not understand a word he said, but his anger was obvious. The hotel owner did not stop pushing the wheelchair. He pushed it as if he had been doing so for years.

Mitzi approached Dr. Langmann, who was walking absorbed in himself, and told him that the night before she had dreamed a very vivid dream. Dr. Langmann, who could not abide idle chatter, averted his long, bald head and said that he too had been unable to sleep because of the dogs. Mitzi told him how when she was still a little girl of five or six her father had taken her to Vienna, to the Prater: it was a wonderful autumn day but her father, a busy, troubled man, only wanted to tire her out before taking her to the hospital to have her tonsils out. When they reached the hospital she sensed the impending catastrophe and tried to escape. All the hospital staff came running. The operation was performed. "And I dreamt it all last night, exactly as it happened."

"The station, the station!" a woman's voice exclaimed. The policemen at the station signaled to the policemen escorting the people.

"We've arrived, we've arrived at last!" cried Mitzi.

35

From the station they could still see Badenheim: a low hill cut like a cone, with the roofs of
the houses like little pieces of folded cardboard.
Only the hotel and bell tower seemed real. The
kiosk owner was delighted to see all the people, and
their eyes lit up at the sight of the lemonade, the
newspapers, and journals—a testimony to the life
that was still going on around them. Dr. Langmann
bought the financial weekly and studied it like a man
returning to a beloved city after years of absence.
His eye fell on some ridiculous item and he laughed
out loud. Sally and Gertie equipped themselves with
two big parcels—one of cigarettes and one of sweets.
The yanuka dirtied his suit and they busied themselves with cleaning it.

The skeptical bitterness did not leave the rabbi's
lips. He placed no faith in these delusions. He had
seen much in his life and all that was left in him was

suspicion, and in this transition too his suspicions did not cease but only grew more intense. The head-waiter bought sausages. The dog liked sausages. The headwaiter's happiness knew no bounds.

The musicians crowded together in a corner, in the shade. Some of the plates had been broken on the way, and they had to unpack their cases and pack them again. This annoying necessity, which gave rise to anger and mutual recriminations, marred the festive atmosphere a little. Strangely enough, Mandelbaum did not despise them. He asked them how they were and inquired about the resorts they played in. His questions relaxed the tension a little.

The people did not forget Samitzky and bought him some bottles of vodka. Samitzky sat on a bench and did not utter a word. "When are we leaving?" asked a woman's voice. Another woman stood next to the closed ticket office and made herself up. Salo put on his old expression again, his traveling sales-man's expression. At any moment, it seemed, he would open his medium-sized suitcase and offer his samples for sale. From here the carriages would pick the people up and there was always the same fra-grance in the air, the fragrance of the transition from the town to the country, and from the station to the enchanted Badenheim. There were no carriages now, but the fragrance still lingered in the air, mingled with an intoxicating dampness.

And suddenly the sky opened and light broke out of the heavens. The valley in all its glory and the hills scattered about filled with the abundance, and even the trembling, leafless trees standing wretchedly at the edge of the station seemed to breathe a sigh of relief.

"What did I tell you?" exclaimed Dr. Pappenheim,

opening his arms in an expansive gesture that seemed too big for him. Tears of joy came into his eyes. All the misery of the days in confinement suddenly burst inside him.

Sally and Gertie wrapped the yanuka up warmly. Karl took the sweater off the bottle: two little fish were already dead and the rest floated limply and listlessly in the water. "Can no one help me?" cried Karl despairingly.

The light poured from the low hills directly onto the station platform. There was nowhere to hide. "Come and see, everybody!" Mitzi suddenly cried, in an affected feminine voice. A little distance away, as if on an illuminated tray, a man was walking with two armed policemen behind him. They came closer as if they were being borne on the light.

"Peter, Peter!" shouted the hotel owner in relief. Peter.

But their amazement was cut short. An engine, an engine coupled to four filthy freight cars, emerged from the hills and stopped at the station. Its appearance was as sudden as if it had risen from a pit in the ground. "Get in!" yelled invisible voices. And the people were sucked in. Even those who were standing with a bottle of lemonade in their hands, a bar of chocolate, the headwaiter with his dog—they were all sucked in as easily as grains of wheat poured into a funnel. Nevertheless Dr. Pappenheim found time to make the following remark: "If the coaches are so dirty it must mean that we have not far to go."

The World of
JOHN
IRVING

"John Irving's talent for storytelling is so bright and strong he gets down to the truth of his time."—New York Times

"John Irving moves into the front ranks of America's young novelists."—Time Magazine

Discover one of America's most exciting writers with these four books, all published in paperback by Pocket Books.

THE WORLD ACCORDING TO GARP
_____ 43996-0/$3.95
SETTING FREE THE BEARS
_____ 44001-2/$3.50
THE WATER METHOD MAN
_____44002-0/$3.50
THE 158-POUND MARRIAGE
_____44000-4/$2.95

POCKET BOOKS
Department JI
1230 Avenue of the Americas
New York, N.Y. 10020

Please send me the books I have checked above. I am enclosing $_____ (please add 50¢ to cover postage and handling for each order, N.Y.S. and N.Y.C. residents please add appropriate sales tax). Send check or money order—no cash or C.O.D.s please. Allow up to six weeks for delivery.

NAME_____

ADDRESS_____

CITY_____ STATE/ZIP_____

169

POCKET BOOKS